A WIND BLOWN TORMENT

Forgotten Gods: Book One

LEAH R CUTTER

Knotted Road Press

A Wind Blown Torment
Forgotten Gods: Book One
Copyright © 2020 Leah Cutter
All rights reserved
Published by Knotted Road Press
www.KnottedRoadPress.com

ISBN: 978-1-64470-132-4

Cover Art:

ID 7838579 © Taily_sindariel | Dreamstime.com

Cover and interior design copyright © 2020 Knotted Road Press

http://www.KnottedRoadPress.com

Come someplace new…
Are you a traveler? Do you enjoy exploring strange new worlds, new cultures, new people?

Journey into the various lands envisioned by Leah Cutter.

Sign up for my newsletter and I'll start you on your travels with a free copy of my book, *The Island Sampler*.

I will never spam you or use your email for nefarious purposes. You can also unsubscribe at any time.

http://www.LeahCutter.com/newsletter/

Also by Leah R Cutter

Forgotten Gods

A Wind Blown Torment

A Stone Strewn Clash

A Sea Washed Victory

Tanish Empire Trilogy

The Glass Magician

The Desert Heart

The Ghost Dog

The Cassie Stories

Poisoned Pearls

Tainted Waters

Spoiled Harvest

Bloodied Ice

The Witch's Progress

Circle of Air

Circle of Water

Circle of Fire

Circle of Earth

Seattle Trolls

The Changeling Troll

The Princess Troll

The Fairy-Bridge Troll

The Troll-Demon War

The Troll-Human War

The Troll-Troll War

The Shadow Wars Trilogy

The Raven and the Dancing Tiger

The Guardian Hound

War Among the Crocodiles

The Clockwork Fairy Kingdom

The Clockwork Fairy Kingdom

The Maker, the Teacher, and the Monster

The Dwarven Wars

The Chronicles of Franklin

Franklin Versus The Popcorn Thief

Franklin Versus The Soul Thief

Franklin Versus The Child Thief

Huli Intergalactic - Science/Space Fantasy

Origins

The Strawberry Girl

Contemporary Fantasy

Siren's Call

The Immortals' War

Chapter One

———————————

WIND

KA LEM CHOSE to spend his first winter's study, after his years of schooling ended, as a female brown bear.

It was a serious task he faced, so he chose a serious animal, ponderous and slow. Besides, his parents, teachers, and various relatives had often told him while he was growing up that he had an old soul, washed more than once in Ishkra's waters to be reborn. Choosing a quick animal, like a cougar, a wolf, or even one of the great horned elk, didn't feel right to him, even though he was only eighteen and most of his friends had taken on such animals.

The first soul animal that one of the Wind People chose to become often tinged the rest of their lives, giving the person some of the traits of that animal. The brown bear was clever, using sticks to dig sweet honey out of a hive, and then using the same sticky tool to capture ants. She knew when to haunt the riverbanks and capture the fish just awakening in the spring, and she always found the best berry patches as well, visiting the same locations year after year.

Ka Lem's teachers approved of his choice. He walked out of the village in his Wind Person form their blessings just after the midwinter celebrations, as the world turned and light began creeping back, the days growing longer. Both moons were full when he started, a good sign. He walked north and east for a week, following farmer roads and the trade routes, and then into the collection paths for the sugar maples. Though he stayed at inns, he didn't see many other travelers along the way: most of the Wind People journeyed as wolves, coyotes, or even pigmy oxen, hurrying down the road and carrying nothing with them. Few would walk as he did, in their Person form, wearing a backpack not just made out of well-oiled cloth but attached to a wooden frame, carrying his belongings with him.

It took time to walk as he did. And though none of the Wind People were as strong as the Stone People, Ka Lim still had broad shoulders and sturdy legs, plus he'd built up endurance that fall helping glean the fields.

The snow crunched under Ka Lem's solid boots and he left a sole trail down the center of the dirt road. In a few months' time, two-wheeled carts would fill the road as the sugar maples were tapped. Then the sap would be collected and hauled off to sugar houses to be boiled off and turned into syrup. Fewer carts would then be needed to take the syrup to market, as much of the sap would be reduced.

Ka Lem hoped that he'd be able to hitch a ride back to his village at that time. For now, he walked in the great cloak his father had given him, made of the hides of *ragyll* sheep, its gray wool twisted into fat lumps that hung on the outside. The cloak would keep out the worst of the winds, as well as the snow and the wet.

A few puffed up chickadees still braved the cold, their chirping cheering him along. Gray skies above the skeletal trees drained the color out of the landscape, making the dark trunks stand out starkly against the white snow. Ka Lem followed his nose as the road finally died and the last of the sugar maples were replaced with pines and firs. He cut under the trees and turned due east, making his steps lighter with his magic so that he stayed on top of the snow instead of sinking hip deep.

His study of the maps of the traders back in his village was soon rewarded, and his feet led him to the edge of a river bluff. Fifty feet below, a white blanket of snow covered the Da Yan River. When Ka Lem listened closely, he could hear the trickle of water still flowing under the ice.

The river was wild this far north, and spring would send huge waves and turbulent water racing along the bank. Further south, though, the waters were tamer and much trade would take place along it.

It took Ka Lem most of the dimly lit afternoon to find, and then climb down, a path over the icy rocks to the cave he'd spotted.

The place was perfect, as he knew it would be. Still, Ka Lem was as cautious as a seasoned hunter. He stood at the mouth of the cave and sent all his senses forward, listening for any sound that would indicate something else had taken residence in this shelter first. He sniffed, but only smelled the musty scent of dried leaves blown by fall winds, not fresh scat. The rock at the mouth of the cave felt dry and cold, and he tasted nothing but dust in the air.

Ka Lem gave a prayer of thanks to Sune Li, the shapeless, formless, ever-shifting god of the Wind People before he took off his pack and rested it beside the entrance. He dug out one of his three wooden torches, its end impregnated with a quick burning oil, and lit it with a match that he carried in his tinderbox.

The brightness of the light made Ka Lem's eyes water. He held the torch far out in front of him as he explored what he hoped would be his winter home. The front of the cave was open and flat, the walls scooped out by ancient spring rains.

He could just stand in the center of the opening, the brown curls at the top of his five-foot three-inch head brushing the ceiling. A narrow passage at the back led to a second "room" that had a shelf on one side and a rounded basin on the floor —probably carved out of the rock by water dripping down the walls in the spring.

Ka Lem went back to the front room and gathered rocks together so he could stand his torch on its end at the entrance to the cave. He didn't try to find dry firewood—he wasn't planning on having another fire for quite some time. Plus, he was afraid the smell of so much smoke would bother the bear he was about to become. Luckily, there was little wind, and the smoke mostly drifted out of the cave.

Ka Lem prepared himself the best he could, stuffing himself with most of the jerked meat he carried in his pack, as well as the dried pears, apples, cherries, and blueberries, as he hummed hymns to Sune Li. He wedged his much-emptied pack between two large rocks, then covered it first with his great cloak and then more rocks, hoping that his scent would keep most creatures at bay. Shivering, he stripped off his sweater and two shirts, followed by his boots, his leggings and trousers, then finally his underclothes, tucking those away under the rocks as well.

He didn't bother with the sacred paints to draw lines across his torso, or paint "fur" across his bare arms. The color of his skin was almost the same as the bear's, as dark brown as a dried oak leaf. The paints weren't necessary to remind him of his own shape or the shape he was about to take. He had stayed in his true form for the past week, that of a person of the Wind People, so he wouldn't be confused about the shape of the body that he would return to.

Ka Lem, like all of the Wind People, could take on the form of any living creature he'd seen in the giant picture books that every child learned from. As a child, he'd played tag with his friends, flitting from one form to the next rapidly, never staying as any animal for more than a few moments.

Today's form was different. It was a soul form. Ka Lem would stay in the shape of a bear from midwinter until spring. The instincts of the bear would drive the body, not the thoughts of the Wind Person. He would truly become a bear, at least for that time.

Like most boys, Ka Lem had wanted to be a brave hunter, until he'd realized how often he'd have to be alone, tracking his prey. When he'd chosen instead to become a teacher, all of his family had approved. As part of his training, over the next three years he would spend many seasons in different soul forms, fully learning that creature. He would also travel to far parts of the world of the Nehuli, visiting the People of Stone and Sea.

Shivering in the cold, Ka Lem called up the form of the female brown bear. The short curly brown hair on his head lengthened, growing down his spine and sprouting across his back and shoulders. The weight of the bear enveloped him, causing him to drop to hands and knees. His face elongated into a snout and wicked teeth sprang up along his jaw.

Ka Lem pulled the soul of the bear around the soul of his being, encasing it in warm animal fur. As he'd been taught, he left a spark of himself outside the soul of the bear, a reminder to awaken once the spring had taken hold, once he heard the sound of the river rushing and the dripping of the melting snow. If he didn't, there was a chance that he'd lose himself, stay in the animal form and never take the shape of a Wind Person again.

The darkness of the winter night overtook him. His thoughts slowed and became essential: No longer full of hymns and words, but instead, full of absolutes, like cold, and dark, and sleep.

He—she—shivered in the cold, shaking her fur and settling it into place. She didn't like the smell of people being so close, or the embers of the fire at the entrance to her cave. But she didn't feel threatened; instead, she understood that the scent would keep out other predators, at least for a little while.

The bear squeezed through the opening at the back of the cave, heading for the smaller space there. She curled up on the hard rock shelf, wishing for more leaves with which to build a nest for herself. But it was too late for that.

She slept and shared her bear dreams with any who would listen.

KA LEM still lay encased in the soul of the bear. But something had woken him. Was it spring?

No, it was midwinter still. Fresh snow covered the top of the hillside and glittered in the light of both moons. Cold winds ruffled the bear's fur as she stretched and growled, throwing her voice to the wind.

Ka Lem had expected the heaviness of the bear to weigh him down, keep him grounded. His teachers had all told him the bear was a wise choice for such a serious young person.

None of them had told him how light a bear was on her feet, how she would sway in the wind or dance spritely over the snow. Her claws raked up flakes with every step, thin clouds of white puffing up behind her as she danced.

All the People danced in celebration of their gods, the Wind People whirling for Sune Li, the Stone People swaying back and forth for Kiproary, and the Sea People flowing around one another for Ishkra.

No one had told him that the animals danced as well, at the joy they found on their feet.

Maybe this bear only danced because Ka Lem lived in the heart of her soul. Or maybe this too was a dream, the bear's thoughts influenced by the Wind Person's hymns.

But the dance had called her from her sleep, the light from the two moons too bright to ignore, even though neither was full.

Though Ka Lem was afraid that he was doing everything all wrong, he still found himself lulled by the bear's movements, falling deeply into her world, the stars above like bright eyes watching the purple-hued snowy mounds, the breeze delicately caressing her fur, the cold in her teeth like a bracing bite.

Winter's grip still tightly clutched the land. She heard/felt it creaking. She knew deep in her bones that the season would last only one more long sleep before it would crack and water and life would come rushing back.

Slowly the bear bowed her head to the night, the winter, and the wind, before she made her way back to her safe warm cave for the rest of her winter's sleep.

A COLD DROP of water on her nose woke the bear yet again. Spring was slowly taking the land. The sound of water rushed beneath her, the river having finally broken free of its ice during the night. Berries and winter fruits were hard to find, most of the bushes already picked clean by birds. Nuts still lay at the base of trees, nuts she could dig through the mushy, wet snow for. The fish wouldn't yet be in the stream, and there were no easy nests for her to pilfer.

The bear rolled over. She should sleep more. Her belly fat would sustain her for a while longer, before she'd be forced from the cave in gnawing hunger.

But something pricked at her consciousness, like the

moonlight that had drawn her out to dance. With a deep growl that echoed across the rock walls, the bear lurched to her four feet. She swayed for a moment before pushing herself through the less-tight opening to the outer room.

A pile of rock to her right caught her eye. She'd been aware of it before. It stank of people, those other than her. She should destroy it, banish the other. Another drop of water splashed on her snout. She growled and shook her head, claws paused in midair. Bright sunlight bounced off the snow outside the cave, blinding her. Maybe she should forage a little, then go back to sleep.

She stuck her head out of the cave, blinking, her thoughts moving slowly. It was too early for her to be up yet.

A loud *boom* echoed off the river bluffs as more river ice broke, losing its grip on the waters it sheltered. The bear shook herself, the sound of the rushing waters sending her blood pulsing.

There was something else she needed to do. She glanced at the stones again. Maybe there was food hidden in there…

Ka Lem found himself rising out of the bear form as she swiped away the rocks covering his belongings. He slid down into himself, sitting naked at the entrance to the cave, shivering in the cold. It was early spring yet, but the bear had been restless.

He'd expected to feel weighed down by the soul of the bear he'd been for the last few months. However, he felt as light as the wind, ready to race across the melting snow. He quickly drew on his layers of clothes, though they all felt stiff and foreign to him, confining after so long of just wearing fur.

However, he was grateful enough for his clever fingers when he opened his pack and got into the remains of the food there. The leathery brown apple rings tore easily, the sweetness making him drool. He licked his fingers free of the salt from the last of the meat. Now, all he needed was water, which was easy enough to come by, given all the snow outside. He filled one of his leather flasks and tucked it under his cloak, knowing it would melt quickly.

Ka Lem gave thanks to Sune Li for guiding and protecting his soul while he'd spent months as a bear. He did, but didn't, feel as different as he'd thought he would. Why would being a bear for so long make him feel so much lighter? As if he wanted to dance? Surely this couldn't be right.

He was a serious young person, who'd just finished a serious study task, learning how to be a bear in his heart and soul.

But no one was there to tell him what was right or wrong, either.

So after Ka Lem finished his meal, he stood and swayed, shuffling from one foot to the other, dancing as the bear had danced in the moonlight, his steps light as he circled the inside of the cave, the soft growls he gave a poor imitation of her magnificent voice.

He would never tell anyone of this dance, just that he'd given praise to Sune Li and the other gods once he'd regained the form of the Wind People.

And he would certainly never tell another soul that he felt, with the certainty of the cold rocks beneath his feet, that the next time there was a full moonrise, with the light of both moons bathing the earth, that he'd feel the call of the bear dance again. Such fancies didn't suit a serious young person like him.

Chapter Two

STONE

NOALANON GLANCED over the heads of zir three children to smile at Jolapen, zir spouse. Ze was making sure the littlest ate at least a couple more mouthfuls of good minerals. The other two were eating steadily, using small spoons that fit their small mouths to clean their bowls.

The five of them all sat together in an eating nook located at one end of the living room. The walls were solid stone, as if carved out of the mountain, though like most modern houses, theirs stood with neighbors on either side, as part of a row. They hadn't painted the walls, but had added a fine coating of quartz and pyrite, so everything sparkled. Flat slate stones, with traces of red, brown, and green, covered the floor, cool and classic looking. Windows at the far end of the room opened up onto a bright, sunny day outside, bringing more cheer to the room.

An oil lamp made out of a beautiful yellowed glass bowl hung from a delicate steel chain over the table, the lit wick giving off a soft light. Though both Noalanon and Jolapen were skilled enough at magic that they could have cast such a light without flame or oil, Noalanon didn't see the point. It was far easier to use materials than energy for simple, mundane tasks.

"Just a little more," Jolapen said, encouraging their youngest, Mathigorn, to eat.

"It's too cold!" Mathigorn complained.

The twins, Kalepef and Turkastein, rolled their eyes and continued to shovel their breakfast in as fast as they could eat it.

Jolapen took the solid stone bowl in zir hands and warmed it. It was one of the special abilities of all the Stone People. They could transfer either heat or cold to any stone.

"There you go," Jolapen said, placing the bowl back down in front of their youngest. "Now, eat your minerals, so you can grow big and strong."

It wasn't that the Stone People ate dirt, though Noalanon had heard that as an ignorant slur more than once, spoken in horror by a visiting Wind Person. The Stone People did eat minerals that came from special mines at the southern foot of the sacred mountain range. In some of the myths of their people, heroes sustained themselves for days on good fertile earth. When Noalanon had been a child, of course ze had tried it for zirself, and had quickly decided that ze wasn't a hero and much preferred the minerals zir parents served instead.

Noalanon had visited homes of both Wind and Sea People, and had marveled at the waste of space that a kitchen took. As the Stone People had no need to cook, they had no kitchens. They did generally have a single shelf with half a dozen large containers for various types of minerals that they mixed together for their meals. In the stories Noalanon and Jolapen recited for their children, kings and very rich merchants would sometimes have entire rooms dedicated to minerals.

When the twins had finished their breakfast, they stood

up together. "May we go?" they asked, their voices eerily similar.

Stone children weren't birthed, not like how the Wind or the Sea People understood the process. Instead, an adult who'd decided to start a family would change zir diet to include a special combination of minerals, then would start to grow what looked like an extra arm out of zir shoulder, or occasionally zir waist. After nine months, the new growth would break off, generally after it had grown to be at least eighteen inches long and at least a foot in diameter.

As soon as the growth detached from the adult, it would transform, the featureless blob molding into head, arms, legs, torso. Every once in a while the form would never gain life and the growth would turn into solid stone instead.

Multiple births were very unusual, though it occasionally happened. Noalanon had birthed the twins, feeling their weight grow ponderous as ze carried them. Together they had been the same length as other children, maybe a little rounder, but Noalanon knew that what ze carried was too heavy to be a single child. Ze alone was unsurprised when the child growth turned into two as soon as they separated from zir.

The twins had similar coloring. While the Wind People were shades of browns and reds, the Sea People pale white with tinges of blue, the Stone People came in many different colors, from the alabaster of pure marble to the gray of solid granite, with all the browns, blacks, and reds in between.

The twins were both a light gray color, like beach pebbles. Fine white lines ran across their skin that would fill in as they aged, their skin growing uniform in color. They both had shocking blond hair that tended to be unruly, though Noalanon hoped that it would darken with age as well. They had the same bright green eyes as ze did, and would probably grow to the same height, just shy of six feet tall.

They'd both grown so fast! Children tended to stay with their parents for two dozen years, until they'd obtained their full height. The twins had just reached their first dozen and were already five feet tall. They looked thinner than the typical Stone Person, who tended to be stocky and solidly built. Though they had just gone through another growth spurt…

"Mana," Kalepef said, calling Noalanon back to the present. "May we go?"

"Yes, yes," Noalanon said. "Though I don't know where you're off to in such a hurry."

The twins grinned at each other but didn't say a word. Ze didn't like the look of mischief in their bright green eyes.

"Thank you Mana, Baba," the two said as they scurried away.

The word *Mana* was generally reserved for the one who carried a child, while the word *Baba* was for the partner. Though Jolapen had carried their littlest one, Mathigorn still called Noalanon Mana as well.

"Can I be done too?" Mathigorn said, looking up brightly at the pair of them.

Mathigorn had similar coloring to Jolapen, a dark gray color like wet slate with straight black hair and blue eyes. Noalanon was much lighter in color, the soft gray of clouds, with the same black hair and green eyes.

"Two more bites," Jolapen directed.

Mathigorn shook zir head, but then scooped up the minerals quickly, shoveling them into zir mouth.

"Chew. Swallow," Noalanon directed before Mathigorn could just take off.

Their youngest didn't roll zir eyes at zir parents. Not quite. But close. Zir was already seven, going on seventeen.

At Noalanon's nod, Mathigorn ran out of the room, possibly going in search of zir siblings and to see what trouble they were getting into.

Jolapen leaned back and grinned at Noalanon, reaching over and taking zir hand. Jolapen's skin felt cool and smooth, the grip comforting and strong. "Just a little while longer," Jolapen said, "before they're all grown and it's just the pair of us again."

Noalanon shook zir head. Ze knew the truth of Jolapen's words, unsurprised that zir mate knew what was going through Noalanon's head, how ze longed for the quiet meals of just the pair of them again.

"I know," ze sighed. "And I do appreciate the time we have together. It's just…"

"I know," Jolapen said. Ze tugged Noalanon closer, wrapping zir arms around zir mate. Noalanon curled in, resting zir head on Jolapen's broad shoulders and zir own arms around zir waist.

"You know, we could take a day of holiday as well," Jolapen said, kissing Noalanon's hair.

"And do what?" Noalanon asked. Ze took a deep breath, smelling the good earth and solid stone scents of zir partner. Though the Stone People weren't known for being flighty, certainly not like the Wind People who were impetuous by their very nature, Jolapen always seemed more steady than most to Noalanon.

"Go explore," Jolapen suggested in a deep voice. "Play."

Noalanon's breath caught. They had always enjoyed each other's bodies, but it had been a long time since they'd taken time off just for themselves.

"I think that sounds like a splendid idea," Noalanon murmured. "As soon as we make sure none of the kids are going to break something, I think we should take a long midmorning stroll."

"You go check on the stonelings. I'll make arrangements for later this morning," Jolapen said after giving zir partner another hug and a long, lingering kiss.

Yes, Noalanon definitely needed to spend some time alone with zir partner. That was one of the advantages of being an adult, after all, the ability to play hooky with each other.

LATER THAT EVENING, Noalanon still found zir eyes drawn back to zir partner again and again. They'd both needed the time together, as well as the release such play granted. Noalanon wasn't sure what ze would do without Jolapen in zir life.

The family was in the living room, sitting on pillows on the floor around the small table in front of the stuffed couch. They played a game with dice, moving their character pieces through a maze painted on a stiff, oiled cloth. The children as well as the adults had to make up a song, poem, or even occasionally dance when they landed on specifically colored squares, which the others got to judge as worthy or not.

The twins tended to vote together, either for or against, though the three children frequently ganged up on one or or the other of their parents. It was a silly game that brought much laughter to all of them.

In the morning, they would all go back to their real lives. The children would be returning to school. Jolapen would go back to laboriously writing up contracts, specializing in land and property deeds. And Noalanon would start training her next group of Wind and Sea People, guiding them through the customs of the Stone People so that they would have an appreciation for one another.

It was a good life, though Noalanon couldn't help but

feel both impatience for this phase to be over, for the next phase of things to take hold, as well as sadness that this part would be over so quickly.

The night sighed around zir, the darkness pressing in.

Noalanon couldn't help but feel as though ze would get zir wish sooner than ze expected.

Chapter Three

SEA

LISETH LISTENED to the young singers, keeping a smile pasted on her face. What the chorale lacked in precision they certainly tried to make up for with enthusiasm.

Two dozen singers had gathered around the base of the statue of Ishkra in the main temple of the capital city of the Sea People, where Liseth served as head priestess. The vaulted ceiling echoed the sweet notes back to the singers, smoothing out some of the more sour ones. They wore their winter holiday best, white shirts with fur or wool collars fluffed out, plain dark trousers and straw sandals.

Liseth sat in the first pew by herself, while the fathers, and sometimes the mothers, of the children filled out many of the pews behind her. The long benches with high backs were beautifully carved out of solid maple wood, golden in color, with graceful scrolls and curves at the edges. A solid brass pole went horizontally across the backs of the bench backs, called a *comfort pole*, and used by those less used to being on land. In the sea, there were no chairs, just poles that people hung onto to keep them in place.

The statue of Ishkra smiled kindly on those gathered at her feet. Liseth had always liked the main statue in the temple, standing twenty-five feet tall and at least fifteen feet at the base. It appeared to be carved out of a single piece of white soapstone, though Liseth knew that the Stone People had actually provided solid granite for the center of the statue and merely a covering of the white stone for her people to carve.

The statue showed the dual nature of the Sea People. The right side was the land-based form, with individual fingers and a smooth neck. The left side was their sea-based form, with prominent gills sticking out of the neck, webbed fingers, and the hint of scales instead of smooth skin.

While the Wind and Stone People could pretend to be each other if they changed their skin and hair color, the Sea People looked much different. They had no hair in either land or sea form. Instead, a bony ridge started at the crown of their head and went back to their necks. Their eyes tended to be spaced wider apart. They grew taller than either the Wind or Stone People as well, usually well over six feet, thin and willowy.

How many years had Liseth listened to young people sing their winter hymns to Ishkra? Not yet thirty, but sometime it felt like over a hundred.

This year had been a long one. Between the fights of the twin capitals—the land city Shiboleth and its sister water city, Sillboden—the fact that the number of births of the Sea People had decreased for the fifth year in a row while the Stone People were having more multiple births than ever before, and that the traditional beds for growing seaweed and other essential crops were producing less, Liseth felt as though she had been fighting a slow, weed-clogged war for most of this year.

And there was no relief in sight, at least as far as she was concerned. She couldn't retire yet. She hadn't found a new replacement, though she needed to start grooming one. Soon, as the high priestesses tended to leave their position when they reached sixty, and she herself was already fifty-two.

But Rygalass, the priestess Liseth had unofficially chosen as her replacement, had died that spring of one of the water-borne diseases. The Sea People were susceptible to more illnesses than either the Wind or the Stone People, with even the slightest cold turning fatal far too often, particularly as they aged.

Liseth knew that it was Ishkra's will for her people to be reborn more often than the Wind or Stone People, that Ishkra called them back more frequently to be bathed in her waters.

But that didn't explain why fewer of the Sea People were being born overall. Or how they were going to grow more kelp and other seaweed that they needed. They were going to have a crisis on their hands come next summer, or the year after that.

Still, Liseth snapped her fingers together as well as made a clicking noise with her tongue to show her appreciation of the singers when they finished. They had no idea of the troubles that lay ahead. They were too young, too precious, the youngest of them barely five years old, while the oldest was maybe twelve.

Their teachers ushered the young singers out of the sanctuary, on their way for spicy tea sweetened with apple juice and cookies. Their parents shuffled out after them, carrying their pride with them. Liseth sat alone in the sanctuary, a chill forming deep in her very bones.

There were too many things to do. Too many arguments that she still needed to have. Too many options in front of her and not enough good or obvious choices.

She needed help. And the goddess, for all her smiles,

wasn't answering any of Liseth's prayers.

LISETH SAT at her desk high in the main tower of the temple complex. The room itself wasn't as fancy as the greeting rooms downstairs. No pearls or beautiful shells were embedded in the walls, no mosaics of sea glass and brilliant stones covered the floor. Instead, the walls were plain whitewashed brick, the floor well-polished wood. Bookcases filled two of the walls, scrolls and important tomes wedged in tightly across the shelves. Liseth's broad wooden desk was covered with books, scrolls, contracts, letters, and papers as well.

A small window let in light to the left of where Liseth sat. The window itself was only a foot wide, though two feet tall. Wavy clear glass covered the opening. While Stone People had a magical gift for working with rock and could shape it without tools, and Wind People could do the same with wood, Sea People worked with glass. Glass workers created mere blobs of unformed glass that the Sea People could then shape and form without having to return it to the furnace.

The primary nod Liseth had given to her position was the beautiful altar to Ishkra that sat in the corner, about a foot tall, carved out of limestone in the shape of an open clam shell with the goddess in her sea form striding forth across the waves. Liseth's chair might also qualify, as it had the feel of a throne, with a high carved back and regal red-and-gold embroidered cushions.

But this was a working office, and Liseth had other rooms where she could meet and entertain dignitaries.

A timid knock at the door made Liseth sigh. "Come in!" she said cheerfully, despite her worries.

Sasuelana poked her head in. "I hope I'm not intruding."

"No, I invited you here. Come in," Liseth said firmly to the other priestess.

Sasuelana scurried across the floor as if afraid something chased her. "How may I serve, my lady?" she asked. She was shorter than most of the Sea People, her skin a beautiful shade of blue-tinged white. The irises in her wide-set eyes were ringed with gold as well as green. She wore a flimsy sleeveless dress in a purple ombre that went from almost white around her face to a dark amethyst color, as well as well-made straw sandals.

She looked ethereal, and she didn't sit completely still, but shifted slightly, as if constantly pushed by gentle waves.

Liseth made herself smile. "I need to start training a new assistant," she said brightly.

Sasuelana nodded. "Brigess might be ready, though she's young," she said. "Or maybe—"

"I was thinking of you," Liseth said, cutting off her assistant's train of thought.

Sasuelana made an inadvertent clicking sound, her surprise obvious. "Me? Why would you consider me?"

Liseth considered her words. "Because you have the most experience," she said. "You know all the players. I wouldn't have to take years educating you on the politics."

The sharp laugh that Sasuelana made surprised Liseth. She hadn't known that her head acolyte could make such a sound.

"No," Sasuelana said.

Liseth blinked and barely avoided making her own clicking noises. "No?" she asked, completely taken aback. Sasuelana was timid about everything. Where had this sudden strength come from?

"I'm almost of an age with you," Sasuelana said. "After you retired, I would only have a few years before I'd have to start training my own replacement. No, you need to start with someone new. Someone fresh out of the water. Then take the time to train them."

"But there is no one," Liseth complained. "No one worthy."

"I'm sure your predecessor said the exact same thing," Sasuelana said. "Even after she found you."

Liseth shook her head. Sasuelana had never spoke so plainly before. "What's gotten into you?"

"I'm planning on retiring before you, my lady," Sasuelana said. "Go and raise my grandchildren. They need me more than you or the city."

"I see," Liseth said slowly. "Are you sure?"

For a moment, the old Sasuelana reappeared, peeking timidly out at Liseth. "No, I'm not. What happens if the crops fail again? I'm afraid without a steady job, my whole family will starve."

"I wouldn't let that happen," Liseth said firmly.

Sasuelana gave her a strange smile. "You wouldn't know." She stood up. "Now, if there's nothing else my lady needs?"

Liseth shook her head. "I could have used such strength before," she said.

"No, you wouldn't have," Sasuelana said with a weary smile. "We would have just clashed like wave and stone. You need to find someone else to beat and break on."

Sasuelana swept from the room without another word, leaving Liseth more alone than usual.

LISETH STOOD at the back of a classroom, her third that week. She'd taken Sasuelana's words to heart and had started looking for younger replacements. She'd started with the teaching and training temples, looking for someone in her early twenties, but couldn't get past the fact that most of the students either thought they already knew everything, or had grown too timid to train.

So she'd started looking at younger children. It wasn't unheard of for a priestess to take on someone who was a teenager. She didn't want to go younger than that—it would take too many years to bring a new priestess on.

Liseth watched the children who flowed through the classroom like a school of fish, always flitting here and there, sitting or standing as they felt the need. She felt sorry for the Stone children, who were forced to sit at their desks for the entire day. Children were meant to move. The Wind People at least understood that, and held most of their classes outdoors.

Though Liseth had been introduced at the start of class, she'd stood as still as coral at the back of the room and most of the children had soon forgotten about her.

The ones who didn't, though, those were who interested her.

It was a girl named Ajooless who caught Liseth's attention that day. The girl was slightly smaller than her classmates, her skin a much darker blue than most, her eyes a single green color. The ridge on her head stood up prominently. She looked awkward, though she moved as smoothly as the others. It was easy to see both land and sea form in her face, as if she were caught somewhere between the two.

What interested Liseth the most was that Ajooless had the appearance of never paying attention to anything the teachers said, yet knew the answer to any question asked. She was also one of the highest performers, particularly when it came to forming her letters and doing her sums. She hid a sharp intelligence behind those sleepy eyes. And she was seventeen, almost an adult.

It finally occurred to Liseth that Ajooless was bored with

class, that she'd already done all the work necessary for that week and was looking for something more challenging.

Well, Liseth could certainly find something much more challenging for her, that was for certain.

Chapter Four

WIND

KA LEM LOOKED with dread at the capital city of the Stone People laid out in front of him. The walls surrounding the city were gray, the houses and roofs were gray, even the streets were gray. It felt to him as if the city had leached all the heat and color out of the very air. The people moved slowly as well, as if they'd all been frozen and were still only partially thawed out.

At least it was summertime. Supposedly. It was never going to get that warm this high in the hills of the sacred mountain. Ka Lem was just going to have to wear extra layers, or else maybe sleep every night in the form of a bear. He wished for a moment that he could emulate one of the great villains in the old stories, like Lan Gi, who, while still in the form of a Wind Person, could also call up fur to keep herself warm.

But spending time living with the Stone People, as well as the Sea People, was part of Ka Lem's training to be a teacher. All of the People regularly exchanged citizens, hosting newcomers in return for their own people being hosted.

A year had passed since Ka Lem had spent the winter as a

bear. He still took on the form regularly. It always surprised him how light he was on his feet since that time. Joy filled his heart when the wind blew and the moonlight of the two moons shone down on him. A secret happiness and lightness took him over that wasn't appropriate for such a serious young person, yet Ka Lem regularly indulged himself in it, at least when no one else was looking.

After living for the summer with the Stone People, Ka Lem would spend the fall in the sacred mountains as one of the great elk who lived there. He'd been planning on taking the form since before he'd first taken the shape of the bear. He would return to the Stone People's city for the midwinter celebrations, then, come spring, he'd travel further west to the capital of the Sea People and spend half a year there. He'd probably transform into some sort of water creature for his training there before he'd retrace his route and finally head back home.

Two years was a long time to be away from his quiet village. He already missed it, missed the wind in the trees and the scent of smoke from the chimneys. Missed the laughter of the children and the wisdom of his parents, though he'd never taken the time to tell them that.

He vowed to tell them how much he appreciated each and every one of them when he returned.

For now, though…Ka Lem shrugged his shoulders, adjusting the sturdy wooden pack that had seen him through so much. He tugged the great cloak around his shoulders more tightly, grimly noting that it would fit right in with the city beneath him, as it, too, was gray colored.

"Quite a sight, yes?" came quiet words beside him.

Ka Lem started. He hadn't heard anyone come up. However, one of the Stone People stood close enough to touch. "It is," Ka Lem said, though he continued to stare at the being beside him.

Ze—not him or her, as the Stone People had no gender —stood taller than Ka Lem by a head. Ze had light gray skin, like snow clouds, with bright green eyes and straight black hair that ze wore long, down past zir shoulder blades. Ze was dressed in a loose green shirt belted over black leggings with solid brown leather boots.

It always surprised Ka Lem that while the Stone People covered their feet, the Sea People didn't. He would have thought the customs would be reversed, but the Sea People always wanted to be able to pour water on their feet, even during the coldest of weather.

"First time here?" the Stone Person asked, still staring at the city below them.

"Yes," Ka Lem said. "I'm spending the summer here."

"At the dormitory?"

"I think so," Ka Lem said. He had an address written down, tucked carefully into his belt.

The Stone Person turned and gave Ka Lem a warm smile. "I am Noalanon," ze said. "I am one of the teachers there."

"I am Ka Lem," he replied, grateful for the introduction. He bowed his head. Though the Wind People, when they met, would grasp arms, he'd been taught that none of the other Peoples did so.

"Greetings, Ka Lem," Noalanon said. "We've been waiting for you. All the others of your class arrived last week."

"Really?" Ka Lem asked, surprised. "I'm not late, am I?" That would never do as a first impression.

"No, the others were all early, eager to get started." Noalanon gave him a sly grin. "I've been coming up to watch the roads to make sure that you wouldn't take one look at Killapany and turn tail and run."

"I would never do such a thing!" Ka Lem protested.

"I'm teasing," Noalanon assured him. "No, your teachers are all quite impressed with you and your diligence."

"Thank you," Ka Lem said, though he wasn't mollified. He couldn't help but sigh as he turned back toward Killapany.

"To your eyes the city appears gray," Noalanon said quietly, zir words barely audible, carried on quiet winds and wrapping around his heart. "You're used to seeing greens and browns, or the golds and reds of fall. While I see an incredible sight, the subtle shading between the walls and roofs, the way the grays mesh and form—it's quite breathtaking."

Ka Lem didn't know how to reply to that. But it was part of why he was here, to learn to see through another's eyes. He diligently searched for the variations Noalanon pointed out, starting to train himself, disappointed that he still couldn't see the beauty that he knew must be there.

"Don't strain your eyes so," Noalanon said after a while. "You'll learn to see the beauty. You may want to come up here once a week while you're staying with us, to continue your training."

"I will," he promised fervently. Given zir smile, Ka Lem wasn't sure if Noalanon was teasing or not. But eventually ze nodded, seemingly pleased.

"Let me escort you to your summer home," Noalanon said. "The others will be happy to meet you."

Ze moved silently forward, walking more smoothly than Ka Lem expected. No wonder he hadn't heard zir come up! He hadn't known the Stone People could move that way.

He had so much to learn! Suddenly, he was looking forward to his time in the city.

Surely a People so quiet on their feet had dances to teach even such a serious young person as he.

KA LEM HUNCHED in his great cloak, happy that Noalanon led the way through the twisted streets to the dormitory. He would have gotten so turned around! Even after asking for directions half a dozen times he would have remained lost.

The coldness of the streets sank deep into his bones. He was afraid that he'd never feel warm again. Leaded window panes filled with glass covered the windows, with sturdy wooden shutters as well. The houses were all in rows, sharing side walls. The doors tended to have rounded tops and were painted in dark colors, green, red, or blue.

The Stone People moved silently through the streets. The only noise Ka Lem caught was the creaking of wheeled carts or the laughter of children. Even the wind seemed hushed down here.

Finally, Noalanon turned a corner and indicated that the dormitory was straight ahead. It was two stories tall, a long flat building.

But most noticeably, there were trees out front. Ka Lem felt his eyes drinking in the greenery. There had been a few trees lining the streets before this, but nothing like the trees in front of him. Those had been tame trees, pruned and trimmed. These trees were wild, the kind that could catch one of the moons in their limbs and call wind storms up to blow their leaves around. They towered over the building behind them, their branches crowning its roof.

Ka Lem couldn't help his sigh of relief when he saw the trees. It meant that it wasn't all stone and cold here. Life and wind could exist here as well.

"My children call this the tree house," Noalanon said. "And there's an orchard out back, as well."

Ka Lem nodded, his throat suddenly growing tight. It was

so kind of the Stone People to have trees here for his people! He was going to have to make sure that the Stone People who came to his village would have just as much comfort, though his village was so small, they didn't regularly have any such visitors.

"More than one new student takes the form of a crow sometimes and spends a night in the trees," Noalanon assured Ka Lem. "There's no shame to it."

He stiffened. He wouldn't need such a crutch. He could survive among the cold and stones.

"Come. Let's get you warmed up and meet your companions for the season," Noalanon said, leading the way again.

Ka Lem sniffed the air as they passed under the trees, the scent of warm bark as much of a homecoming as anything else.

He wouldn't need to spend a night out there, tucked in among the leaves. At least, not yet.

KA LEM STOOD in front of the dormitory, shivering in the rough fall winds, thinking back on the summer that had now passed. Noalanon stood beside him, zir delight in the world still apparent. Ka Lem had expected that the Stone People would be solemn and stiff. He'd been so wrong!

While being a bear had left Ka Lem feeling lighter than he imagined, being with the Stone People had left him less grounded, less connected to the earth. They lived in light and shadow, gliding across the ground. They could turn motionless as a stone, and they could disguise themselves, hiding in plain sight, completely camouflaged against a variety of backgrounds. Though the Wind People could take any shape, the Stone People could take on any colors and variation, including patterns such as brick. It was a useful disguise for children who were playing games.

The most powerful of their magic users could also cast illusions, fooling the eye into believing something was there or not there, such as a chair or a wall, even a deep crevice in the earth.

Ka Lem had enjoyed his time with the Stone People more than he'd originally thought he would. Now, however, it was time for his next soul shape. Ka Lem planned on flying into the foothills of the sacred mountains instead of walking there. He'd decided that he was firmly enough grounded that he could take a chance and fly for a brief while before taking on his next soul shape.

"Thank you," Ka Lem said again, reaching out to grasp arms with Noalanon.

Ze gave him an indulgent smile and clasped his forearms with zir cool, strong grip. "And thank you, in return, for sharing your spirit with us."

Of all Ka Lem's teachers, he'd grown closest with zir, even meeting zir spouse and children. It astonished him how similar, yet how different, their People were.

"Be sure to give my best to Jolapen and your children," Ka Lem said, giving Noalanon's arms a final squeeze.

"I will," Noalanon said. "Now, be off with you. Time for your next great journey."

Ka Lem nodded. He wasn't sure why he felt so hesitant to start. He'd be returning here in a few months, after spending the long fall as one of the great elk who wandered the nearby mountains.

He bowed his head to Noalanon again, then shrank his form down, compacting himself into a huge eagle, four feet tall with a massive wingspan. With a loud caw, he threw himself at the air, seeking fresh winds and mountain peaks.

He wouldn't need his backpack or coat. He'd left those with Noalanon for the season.

As this wasn't a soul form, Ka Lem still had most of his Wind Person senses and sensibilities. It was a delicate balance between the animal instincts and the Wind Person thought processes. If he brought too much of his own sensibilities forward, he'd fall in midair, plummeting toward the ground. If he let the bird have too much control, he might not make it to his destination.

Ka Lem circled the foothills, searching for the great elk. He found their trails but he never saw any herds. Very strange. The eyes of the eagle were strong enough to seek out the clambering sheep and goats, had even spied a mountain lion as well as flushed many smaller animals who would have been perfect for prey.

But no elk. Had they migrated to lower ground? Or were they higher up in the hills? He wasn't sure which way to look.

Eventually, Ka Lem landed at the base of what he was certain was a trail leading through a dense forest. Surely, somewhere along this path he'd run into one or more herds. He shivered in the fall winds, naked on the cold mountain. He couldn't stay in his Wind Person form for long, not without damage to his body.

Ka Lem bowed and gave a brief prayer to Sune Li, then he tried to pull the form of the elk over his soul.

It felt as though he reached into an empty cave, with nothing there, nothing to hold onto. There was no elk form there for him to find.

Ka Lem opened his eyes and looked around, confused. The elk had to be nearby. And Ka Lem could take any form he'd learned about.

His failure wasn't because he'd been the form of an eagle earlier, was it?

No. He couldn't fail.

Ka Lem reached again for the form of an elk. He hummed a song of the Wind People that praised all the animals, reciting the verse about the shaggy elk, with his huge rack of antlers and sturdy hooves.

Still, Ka Lem couldn't find the form of an elk, couldn't reach the soul of the animal.

Did he need the sacred paints? Should he have walked into the mountains? What was wrong? Ka Lem dropped onto his hands and knees in anticipation of changing form, but he couldn't bring up the soul of the elk. His head remained human, no antlers sprouted up, his skin stayed smooth and covered in goosebumps.

Shaking his head, Ka Lem reached for another form in desperation.

The form of a regular deer came easily to him, both the male form with antlers as well as the doe. He felt his legs elongate and his knees shifted direction, a fine brown coat covering his skin. His eyes spread to the sides and color drained out of the world.

From there, he tried again to reach for the elk, either the male or the female form.

It continued to feel as though he were reaching into an empty hole, as if the soul of the elk had been scooped out of the world.

Ka Lem flickered through half a dozen other forms: bear, wolf, coyote, mountain lion, goat, sheep, and even wild dog. He hadn't lost his ability to change form.

But there were no elk, none that he could reach.

He thought back to how strange it had been that he hadn't found any elk on the mountain. It was as if they'd all been herded away.

Trembling, Ka Lem returned to the form of a great eagle. He would find where the elk had gone, flying all the way back to the lands of the Wind People if need be.

Chapter Five

STONE

NOALANON WAS grateful for a week off after the last class of Wind and Sea People who had visited. Ze had enjoyed the most recent class very much. Particularly Ka Lem, such a serious young person who ze couldn't help but tease constantly.

The next group would be just as special in their own way, though. Noalanon needed the week break to help zir let go of the previous group, so that ze would take the next group as it was and not be constantly comparing them either favorably or unfavorably with the previous group.

Noalanon spent the first three days at home, tending their house, applying a new coat of phosphorous to the ceiling in the children's rooms so that the ceiling glowed as if covered in faint stars when the children went to sleep. Ze had other projects as well, sewing on buttons and mending rips, darning socks and planning out their winter holidays.

However, as usual, by the third day, Noalanon was looking forward to working again, to being out of the house. Ze spent the morning at the market, acquiring a few more ounces of the minerals zir children needed to grow strong and healthy, taking zir time to talk with the merchants, eventually buying zirself a soft shawl woven out of the most beautiful dyed red flax.

Around noon ze returned to their house, unsure how exactly ze was going to fill up the afternoon hours. A loud caw startled zir as ze opened the door. Ze paused, looking around. With a *whoosh*, a huge eagle landed behind zir.

"Ka Lem?" Noalanon asked, surprised. What was he doing here? Why was he here? Had something gone wrong?

The huge eagle shook itself, shrinking down and in, as the torso expanded up, turning into the young person Noalanon knew as Ka Lem. It was such a remarkable transformation. It always took Noalanon's breath away to watch.

But zir joy quickly fled. Ka Lem stood naked before zir, shaking. His brown skin had a pale sheen to it, as if he'd been washed in white ash. His curly brown hair stood up all around his head like a wild mane. Terror filled his brown eyes.

He didn't bother covering his male parts with his hands. The Wind People had no taboo about being naked. As the Stone People had no breasts or other sexual organs, they also had no taboo about being naked. It was only the Sea People who found it distasteful.

"What is it? What's wrong?" Noalanon asked, walking forward.

Ka Lem shook his head. "There are no elk," he said. His voice sounded as hoarse as if he'd been screaming for days. "They've been taken away. Stolen."

"What?" Noalanon said. "What are you saying?" How could there be no elk? It was inconceivable that an entire species of animal be just…taken.

"I can reach every other animal," Ka Lem said. "I can change into every other form. But not the elk."

A whirling cloud appeared to be circling Ka Lem as he switched rapidly from one form to another, bear, eagle, lion, wolf, deer, sheep, goat, dog, and back to Wind Person. "All the other forms are there. All the other creatures are there. I circled the mountains three times. I searched high and low. But the elk are gone. Missing."

"Come inside," Noalanon said, "before you freeze to death." While ze thought the day was very pleasant, and wore merely a shirt and light trousers, ze was aware that the Wind People would find the air very chilly indeed.

The manic energy that appeared to be driving the young Wind Person drained away. Ka Lem stumbled into the front room after zir. Noalanon grabbed blankets for him and installed him on their couch where he sat, shivering. Ze got one of their good stone mugs, filled it with clear water, then wrapped zir hands around it, warming it before handing it to Ka Lem.

"Thank you," he said through chattering teeth.

"What has you so cold?" Noalanon asked. Ze didn't try to touch the Wind Person, as ze knew zir touch would be perceived as cool, not warm.

"That place where the elk should be," Ka Lem admitted after a few moments, taking several sips of the hot water. "It's colder than a grave. No life left there. No breath. Just death."

"I'm sorry," Noalanon said automatically, unsure of what else to say. "What do you think happened to the elk?"

Ka Lem shook his head and shivered. "I don't want to speak it out loud. I'm afraid it will make it so."

"Speak and be heard," Noalanon instructed. "We cannot fix that which we cannot see." Zir words had a ritualistic formality to them that ze didn't care for, but ze couldn't help it.

This had been one of zir students. Ze was still a teacher. Ka Lem was still zir responsibility.

"I dreamed…I dreamed of the elk. Or rather, the last of the elk," Ka Lem said. His voice broke. He cleared his throat and tried again. "He'd been killed, and his great rack of antlers scalped from him. The meat and fur, even the entrails, had been discarded, heaped in a stinking pile to the side, while the bones had been carefully cleaned."

Ka Lem's disgust at such waste was apparent. The Wind People used every part of any animal their hunters killed.

"A person stood there, male. Tall, with long straight black hair, like a Stone Person. But his skin wasn't gray. It was white. He'd strung the bones of the elk together with cruel wire and chains, then hung them from his shoulders like a great cloak. But the skull…the skull…"

Ka Lem gulped another draught of water, as if trying to prevent himself from vomiting.

"The pale person had also wired the antlers to the skull of the elk, that he wore over his own face. But the antlers were backwards! Instead of gracefully reaching across the person's back, they poked forward, awkward. They made the person unbalanced. The bones clicked in the wind as the person started his dance."

Ka Lem's voice took on more fear and horror, cracking with pain. "He transformed, like one of the Wind People. Only instead of taking on the full form of the elk, he became only the skeleton. He walked stiffly, the joints grinding together, his head dipping again and again, the backwards antlers throwing him off balance. Then, then…"

Ka Lem put down the cup of water onto the small table in front of the couch, as if afraid that his shaking would spill what little water remained.

"Then he transformed completely. I don't know how else to describe it. It was as though he suddenly took on the soul form of the elk, his own soul completely encased by the dead. He grew *graceful,* in a horrible, macabre way.

And his eyes changed. They grew red. Burning. What they gazed on caught fire. The field of dried grass that he stood in started to smoke. The pines that grew on the edges lit up like torches, the tops burning fiercely. Everything started to burn around him, and then he started to dance again."

All the emotion fled from Ka Lem's voice. "He danced a dance of the dead. Only not to lay them to rest. To awaken them. To bring back all the dead so that he could devour them again."

Noalanon swallowed against a dry throat. "It was just a dream," ze said hoarsely. "It wasn't real. Was it?"

Ka Lem shivered one more time abruptly, then collapsed further into the blankets piled around and over him. "I don't know. But I fear…I fear that's where the elk have gone. To feed this creature. To bring him strength. So that he can do it again. With the deer, or the goats, or the sheep, or some other creature. To gain more strength. To devour everything. To burn the world down."

Noalanon took a deep breath. "We will stop him," ze said firmly.

"But how?" Ka Lem said plaintively, sounding as young as one of zir children. "How do we stop the dead from claiming their own?"

"I don't know," Noalanon said. "We don't know for certain that is what's happening. It may be just a dream. We need to find other Wind People. See if they can find the elk."

"Then let's go," Ka Lem said, struggling to stand.

"No," Noalanon said. "Rest first."

Ka Lem gave a strangled laugh. "I can rest when I'm dead," he said.

Noalanon couldn't help the shiver that came over zir. Normally, the Stone People never really felt cold or heat, as they could adjust their internal temperatures and always feel comfortable. But to zir, a cold wind had just blown thrown the living room, one that ze wasn't sure would ever go away.

NOALANON WASN'T friends with any Wind People who lived in Killapany permanently, but ze did know several of the merchants. Ze often bargained with them, buying treats from "home" for zir students.

Ka Lem had dug into the pack he'd stored at Noalanon's and pulled out some of his clothes, as well as his great cloak. Noalanon felt as though the gray cloak suited him better than it ever had before, as if a gray fog still whirled around him, the cold winds of the mountain following him through the crowded streets.

Noalanon took them directly to Gan Ou, one of the merchants who sold beautiful knit scarves and shawls all year round. She usually was gone for a couple months during the spring to travel back to the border of the lands of the Wind People and pile her cart high with raw wool that she'd spend the rest of the year spinning, dying, and turning into wearable art.

Gan Ou was one of the most dour people Noalanon knew. Some bitter tragedy followed her, making her corner of the market seem gray, despite her colorfully dyed goods. She had the face of a dried apple, light brown and full of wrinkles, with a mouth that only knew how to frown.

However, Noalanon also knew Gan Ou to be the most grounded Wind Person ze had ever met. Gan Ou always had her feet firmly on the solid stones beneath her.

The market place smelled of the sweet beeswax of sacrificial candles, dried lavender for pillows and sachets, and tanned leather goods. When Noalanon had been younger, she'd traveled to markets of both the Sea and Wind People, and had always marveled at how many of the booths had been dedicated to cooked foods and ingredients. Those foreign markets had smelled so differently.

"Gan Ou," Noalanon called out as they approached.

The Wind Person looked up from her knitting and hrumphed. "What sort of charity are you looking for today, Noalanon?" Gan Ou said.

Noalanon held up her hand to stop Ka Lem from saying anything in zir defense. Gan Ou was just like that, always poking at people.

"We have a perplexing problem," Noalanon said smoothly. "One that we're hoping your wisdom can help with."

"Hmmm," Gan Ou said. She placed her knitting down on the top of the table with a thump. "What trouble has this youngster gotten into now?"

"Ka Lem is not in any trouble," Noalanon said smoothly. "But he needs your help. He can't find the soul of the elk anymore."

"Too lazy to study your forms, eh?" Gan Ou challenged, looking Ka Lem up and down and obviously forming a bad opinion of the young Wind Person.

"No, he's quite studious," Noalanon said quietly, raising her hand again to keep Ka Lem from replying. "But the form of the elk has disappeared."

"Nonsense," Gan Ou said.

"Can you find it?" Ka Lem challenged.

"Of course I can," Gan Ou said immediately.

Ka Lem raised his chin at her in defiance. "Can you?"

A look of puzzlement crossed Gan Ou's face. "Of course," she repeated. She blinked, her face growing blank for a moment. "What devilment is this?"

Ka Lem took a step back and crossed his arms over his chest. "Find the elk."

Gan Ou shook her head and stood slowly. "I will, just to prove you wrong."

Noalanon was surprised at the strain that filled the older person's face, as if she were struggling to lift a heavy weight. "They're…they aren't there," she said after a moment. Sweat broke out across her wrinkled brow. Her dark eyes grew wide with fear. "Where are the elk?"

Ka Lem started trembling again. "I don't know," he said hoarsely. "But you can't find them either?"

Gan Ou shook her head. Suddenly, she transformed into a great wolf, weighed down with the old person's clothing. Then a huge horned ram, a giant eagle, finally back into the old person's form again, shifting her clothes back around so she wore them properly.

"The elk are missing from the world," Gan Ou whispered. "How is that possible?"

"I don't know," Ka Lem said. "But we have to find whoever did it, and stop them. Before they do it again."

"What…what should we do?" Gan Ou asked, her voice sounding as weak and trembling and as old as her face.

"Can you make it back to the elders? Quickly? Warn them of what has happened? I will go forward to the Sea People, to ask them what they know," Ka Lem said.

Gan Ou nodded. A sudden smile creased her face, appearing to split it into two. Noalanon had never seen such an expression on the old person before. "The elders *must* speak with me now, despite my banishment." She gave a cackling laugh. "Perhaps I can redeem myself before I face Ishkra and her waters."

Before Noalanon could ask what she meant, Gan Ou shrank down into nothing. Her clothing collapsed, as if they'd been supported by a bubble that had suddenly burst. Beside the heap of clothes, a tall gray form appeared, that of a great peregrine falcon, three times the size of those generally found in the mountains.

She cawed twice at Ka Lem, who nodded as if he understood. Then Gan Ou leaped into the air, her loud caws sending shivers down Noalanon's spine.

"She's gone to speak to your elders?" Noalanon asked as Ka Lem turned to face her.

"Yes, back to Shan Yu, the capital," Ka Lem said. Then he shook his head. "No, I don't know what she did to disgrace herself, to get herself banished from the lands of the Wind People. But the elders will listen to her, particularly since she dared to come back." He sighed. "I'm to go to the Sea People, to warn them, and to see what they know."

"Do you want company?" Noalanon asked, surprised at zirself for offering.

Ka Lem paused, considering. "I will get there faster flying on my own," he said after a moment. "And you need to tell your council here of the news." He paused, then added, his words ringing like the bells at a funeral. "And prepare for the worst."

Chapter Six

SEA

LISETH HEARD the great cawing even from inside her study. Some massive bird had just landed on the roof of the temple and was making a racket louder than the temple bells.

She'd spent most of the afternoon with Ajooless, finally feeling as if she were making progress there. All of the child's teachers had warned Liseth away from the girl, saying that she wasn't well suited to a position of power. They knew that she was smart, but she was also disrespectful.

Secretly, Liseth thought that would make the girl a better leader. Too many of the Sea People were diffident, trained from birth to put others' wishes before their own. Like Sasuelana, they wouldn't stand up to Liseth or anyone else, trying to achieve a coalition of opinions instead of leading when they needed to.

She often saw that with the council of regents. Over a century before, the Sea People had been ruled by a monarchy. However, a series of plagues had wiped out the entire royal family. Ever since, they'd been ruled by a council of six regents, three from the land city, three from the sea city. The positions were hereditary. Liseth was not a regent, but as the high priestess, she was on the council and had an equal vote. She often acted as the tie breaker.

As much as Liseth wished, she couldn't just order Ajooless to take her new responsibilities seriously. The girl had a tendency to treat everything like it was a game, as well as beneath her. She hadn't appreciated the honor that Liseth was trying to bestow on her.

Ajooless was finally starting to appreciate the politics involved between the land and sea capitals, and instead of being impatient dealing with the others, was beginning to learn the art of diplomacy.

That afternoon, just when Liseth had settled in behind her desk to drink a little spiced tea and relax while reading the latest kelp farm reports, this damned bird came squawking and interrupting her.

It had to be one of the Wind People. Normal birds that size didn't just land on a tower and start calling for attention.

With a sigh, Liseth put her tea to the side and marched out of her office, up the winding steps of the tower to where the stupid bird had installed itself.

Liseth didn't employ guards at the temple. They weren't necessary. If someone had need, all they had to do was ask. The Sea People knew poverty, certainly, all the various Peoples did. But no one went without the basics of food and shelter. Ishkra would turn her back quickly on those who didn't reach out with the open hand of hospitality.

The wind blew cold from the sea that afternoon, winter carried in its teeth. Unlike the Wind and Stone People, the Sea People rarely saw snow in their lands, particularly not this close to the water. Warm currents kept the kelp beds alive year round and brought warmer winds.

Liseth knew the view from up on top of the tower was pretty, though she rarely came up here to admire it. Much of the capital had either been built from white stone or had been whitewashed. It gleamed even in the pale sunlight, a pearl nestled in between the green hills to the east and the gray waters to the west. Many of the roofs had been formed out of red clay tiles, a stark contrast that highlighted the dual nature of all the sea folk, as well as their goddess, who represented life as well as death, who was prayed to both during childbirth and at funerals. Thin clouds spread across the cool blue skies, yet another reminder of the changing season and the coming winter.

The bird clutched the edges of the tower roof with wicked, black talons protruding out of scaly yellow feet. Golden brown feathers covered its head, neck, and upper chest, while darker brown feathers spread across its wings, giving it the appearance of being bathed in sunlight. Its eyes were like liquid gold, staring mercilessly at her, while its beak was the same bright yellow as its feet.

"I am Liseth, the head priestess of the temple of Ishkra," she announced to the bird, standing her place. She had no defenses against the thing, but it didn't look sick or diseased.

She knew that Sasuelana and the others were likely cowering someplace, maybe praying loudly at the feet of the goddess, asking for deliverance.

The bird nodded to her, as if it understood. It hopped off the roof and onto the solid ground of the balcony. Liseth took an abrupt step back. The stupid thing wasn't about to attack her, was it? She could move quickly enough if it did, flowing around it like water. However, she had no armor, sword, or bow. Nothing she could defend herself with.

The creature shook itself, then rapidly shrank in, its feathers transforming into skin, its torso straightening out. A Wind Person stood in front of her, obviously male. He had dark brown skin, curly brown hair, and wild brown eyes.

"I've come to warn you," he said, his voice harsh, as if he hadn't used it in a while. "The elk have vanished."

Liseth blinked. She tried to understand the significance of what he was saying. "What do you mean, the elk have vanished?"

"They've been taken," he growled.

Liseth blinked, unease stirring her soul. "Come inside and tell me your news." She turned abruptly and walked back inside the temple, expecting the person to follow.

She didn't understand what it meant that the elk had vanished, but she knew it couldn't be good.

THE WIND PERSON–KA Lem—sat enveloped in the blue and gold temple robes that Liseth had found for him. As the Sea People were generally at least a foot taller than the Wind People, he almost looked like a child.

Almost. His eyes, and the dark terror they still held, gave him away.

He had his hands wrapped firmly around the mug of spiced tea that she'd served him, sipping its warmth as if he were drawing from it the strength to continue.

He'd told her of how the elk had vanished from the world, how neither he or other Wind People could find that form anymore. Then he'd told her of his dream, of the person who wore the bones of the elk and transformed into a creature who fed on the dead.

"This person—these Bone People," Liseth said, giving a name to them, "where do they come from?"

Ka Lem shook his head. "I don't know. I don't even know if they're real. It may have only been a nightmare."

"You wouldn't have told anyone if you truly believed that," Liseth said, dismissing his hesitation.

Ka Lem gulped audibly, then nodded. She'd judged him to be a serious young person, not given to fanciful stories.

"Do the Bone People come from the north? From the east? From the south?" she asked.

Ka Lem thought for a moment. "Not from the north," he said after a moment. "Ice and snow fill those lands. Also, if the Bone People came from the north, wouldn't they have taken the great white bear and not the elk?"

"That makes sense," Liseth said. "And the elk don't travel far that far to the south, do they?"

Ka Lem shook his head. "It grows much warmer south of the lands of the Wind People."

"Same with the Stone and Sea People," Liseth said. The Sea People's lands actually ended at the mouth of a great river that emptied out into the sea. There had always been talk of colonizing the southern bank of the river, but with the falling birthrates, there hadn't been need.

The Stone People lived along the mountain ranges that dominated the center of their territory. However, the mountains petered out eventually to the south, giving way to jungle, an environment the Stone People weren't comfortable.

"So what lies east of the Wind People?" Liseth asked after a moment.

Ka Lem blinked. "There's a river," he said, hesitatingly. "And flatlands. Prairies, meadows, lakes. Not as many forests. My People have never really spread that far east or south. There hasn't been need."

"Maybe the Bone People come from beyond those prairies," Liseth speculated.

"I'm sure the elders will send scouts that way," Ka Lem said, nodding. He seemed to be a little more relaxed when he thought of that. "But why have the Bone People come this way? What do they seek?"

Liseth paused before she answered. "What do you know of how the world was created?"

Ka Lem shrugged. "You mean how Sune Li formed the first companions out of the dark formlessness? Gan Zhur and Ban Zhur?"

"No," Liseth said. She couldn't help but smile, her tone changing to that of a teacher. "That's the Wind People's version of creation. Are you familiar with the Sea People's version?"

Ka Lem screwed up his face and thought for a moment. "Ishkra gave birth to two sets of People before us? And that this is the third age, that of the Wind, Stone, and Sea People?"

"Exactly," Liseth said. "We all know that the gods watch and wait, lest the People forget themselves. If any of the People decide to challenge the gods, this age would end in fire and all the People, with the help of the gods, would die."

Ka Lem looked alarmed. "That's really what you believe?"

"It is what we're taught, yes," Liseth said. "And this new People. The Bone People. They're challenging the gods."

"What do you mean?"

"The dream you had—the person is seeking more death. Death is the province of Ishkra, and hers alone. If they are bringing death to entire species, the gods will not stand idly by. There will be war, and we will lose," Liseth said firmly. "This age will end. All the People will die. It will be the will of the gods."

Ka Lem's eyes grew even rounder. "We must stop them," he whispered hoarsely. "The Bone People."

"First, we must find them," Liseth said. "But we cannot go to war with them. The gods will turn their backs on us if we go to war. We must stop the Bone People without fighting them."

Ka Lem shook his head. It was obvious he didn't agree with her assessment. The Wind People were much rougher than any of the other People. They had summer games where they competed with each other, races, hunting, wrestling, and fighting. They were much more likely to go to war than the other people, though none of the three peoples had warred either with each other or among themselves for many decades.

"I will send scouts out, up through all the rivers," Liseth said.

Ka Lem looked confused. "What do you mean?"

"Only the Wind People have the ability to pick any form," Liseth said, easily falling into teaching mode. "We can only change between our land and sea forms. We cannot become a fish or a whale."

Ka Lem nodded. He'd learned this when he'd started training to be a teacher.

"However, the Sea People can see out of the eyes of a water creature. Most no longer have the ability, but a few have retained it," Liseth said with pride.

"Really?" Ka Lem asked, fascinated. "We have myths where the great heroes could talk with the birds, find out what they saw, though no one has that ability today."

Liseth nodded. She'd heard those same myths and wondered if the Wind People had, at one point, had a similar ability to that of the Sea People. "We also know the waters. We can trace a single drop in a mighty stream back to its humble beginnings. If the Bone People are anywhere near water, we can find them."

"Then I will stay here until you hear back from your scouts," Ka Lem announced, "before I return to first the Stone People, then the Wind People."

"We may not be able to find the Bone People," Liseth warned. "They may be avoiding all flowing water, sticking with still lakes instead. That would make it much more difficult to find them."

"The Wind People will be searching as well," Ka Lem said. "We will find them."

Liseth nodded. She knew that her people had to find the Bone People first.

Or else there would be war.

LISETH STOOD before the six regents, telling them the news from Ka Lem. Ajooless stood behind her, to the right, in an attendant's position. Liseth felt the girl's eyes boring into her back, as if trying to absorb not only the words Liseth spoke but every single nuance of meaning.

The council chamber itself was round, with the ceiling rising to a dome. The walls were painted a subtle brown-gold, supposedly to indicate the wisdom of those gathered here, while the ceiling was blue, green, and gray, with a suggestion of waves and currents flowing across it. Ancient tapestries hung from the walls, muting the hard stone, showing images of the long dead royal family, as well as fanciful stories of the heroes and beings of legend. The wood table the regents sat at was round, so that no one sat at the "head" or considered themselves most important.

Liseth kept her face neutral, trying not to radiate satisfaction when the regents all looked appropriately shocked and worried. They pledged her whatever resources she needed in order to find the Bone People, to get their ambassadors to them, to stop any coming war.

What did the Bone People want? How could the Sea People bargain with them? Were they really trying to challenge the goddess? There were too many unanswered questions.

One of the teachers at the main temple had the best fish sense of any of the acolytes that Liseth could find. The person searched upstream as rapidly as she could, leaping from one mind to the next, teasing out what had been seen, looking for any hint of a new People who had crossed the waters or dipped their hands into a stream.

Ka Lem remained in the teacher quarters, sleeping much and regaining his strength. When he was awake, he peppered the instructors there with questions, absorbing as much as he could about the Sea People and their culture.

"So how do we stop the Wind People from warring on the Bone People as soon as they're found?" Regent Ruschyard asked. "We all know how impetuous the Wind People can be. Like children, really."

Liseth knew that the Wind People weren't necessarily that bad, they did have that reputation, while the Sea People had always considered themselves the wisest of the three Peoples.

"What if the Bone People are trying to challenge the goddess?" Regent Solangess said.

"Why would they do that?" Regent Abrassis said. "The world will be destroyed if they do. All the people will die."

"Maybe they want to bring about the next age," Liseth said quietly. Why else would someone want to challenge the gods?

"Are they insane?" Regent Abrassis said.

"We know nothing of them, nothing of their lives or their myths," Liseth said. "We didn't even know they existed before this."

"They can be bargained with," Regent Ruschyard said. "We just have to figure out what they want."

Of all the regents, Liseth worked best with Regent Ruschyard. She had strong roots in the merchant community, her feet washed by trade and commerce.

Liseth could only hope that Regent Ruschyard was correct this time.

After Liseth and Ajooless left the council chambers, they

walked through the quiet streets of Shiboleth, on their way back to the temple complex. Cobblestones covered the ground, worn flat in ruts where decades of wagon wheels had passed. The windows of the buildings edging the street were shuttered, though candlelight and firelight seeped out through the cracks and around the edges, giving the houses a warm glow.

Liseth had called up a slight light that she sent floating above them so that they could make their way through the darkened city. More than one regent had proposed additional lights in the land city, but no one else had ever seen the need to fund it. Most of the Sea People had the ability to call up a simple phosphorous ball, bright enough to see by. The water city needed the light to scare away larger fish and predators who might have thought the people there were easy prey.

At the intersection of two of the main streets a small fountain splashed merrily. Without thinking, Liseth walked up to it directly and stuck first one foot, then the other, under the flow. It was traditional with the Sea People to wash their feet frequently. It was partly a symbolic gesture, of washing away the cares of the day. It was also quite soothing for the Sea People to wet their feet. Whenever people argued, one or the other might be told to go wash their feet to help them cool their tempers.

When Liseth realized that Ajooless hadn't joined her, she beckoned the girl to come up and do the same.

"What is it?" Liseth said. She could tell that the girl wanted to talk, to maybe ask something.

"What can I do to help?" Ajooless said quietly as she stuck her feet, one after another, into the fountain. "It feels like such a big task, to be facing an unknown People who might be challenging the gods."

Liseth nodded, taking it as a good sign that Ajooless

actually wanted to help. "What do you know about tracing the waters?"

Ajooless screwed up her face as she thought. Liseth allowed the girl that "tell" for now, though at some point, she'd have to become more inscrutable.

"I was just starting to learn how to taste the waters," Ajooless said slowly, nodding. "To distinguish one stream from the next."

"Good," Liseth said, approving. "That's what I want you to work on. Keep tracing the waters upstream. Keep going back to the sources of the waters, half a continent away. We need to be able to find the homelands of the Bone People. It will mean following underground streams and aquifers, as there aren't many rivers that actually travel east-west, most go north-south. But that is our best hope of stopping them."

Ajooless nodded. "I will do my best," she promised. "Every night, before I go to sleep, I will explore a bit further upstream and across the continent."

"Thank you," Liseth said sincerely. She doubted that the girl would find anything that her scouts and other trained searchers wouldn't find first. She still took it as a good sign that the girl wanted to help, and was pledging her aid.

Liseth didn't bother telling Ajooless what the Sea People might do once they found the headwaters of the Bone People. Very few had the ability to develop a water-born plague, particularly in lakes and streams so far away. It would be extra tricky, as any crafted disease needed to be done in complete isolation, so that the originator wouldn't accidently infect those nearby.

However, working in concert, a group of the Sea People might be able to set off a plague among the Bone People, to stop the war before it even started.

Chapter Seven

WIND

GAN OU CIRCLED the capital of Shan Yu, still in the form of a giant eagle. She could hardly call the place a city. It really was just an overgrown village. The streets were all dirt and gravel, not paved. One-story houses and wooden huts filled the area, not grand stone buildings or temples. Gardens took up most of the yards instead of statues and stone paths.

Yet, the sight still filled her heart with gladness. Even as winter approached, there was more green in this city than in all of Killapany, the capital of the Stone People where she'd lived for over forty years.

Would the elders still remember her? Would any of the ones who'd banished her still be alive? She'd been barely eighteen when she'd accidently killed her opponent during a wrestling match at the summer games that year. Gan Ou hadn't been able to show much remorse, at least not enough that the elders trusted her not to kill again.

Gan Ou had never explained that both she and her opponent had been in love with the same boy. Then, her opponent had gone out of her way to break Gan Ou's heart and steal him away.

Did he still live somewhere in Shan Yu? She'd never kept track of him, taking the punishment on her own, feeling as though it was justified, despite her age and circumstances.

She cawed loudly as she circled, drawing the attention of those outside. They pointed at her and whispered among themselves.

Finally, someone had the smarts to enter into the building where the elders gathered, to draw their attention.

Only after three of the elders had walked into the cold morning light did Gan Ou descend to the earth.

While Gan Ou could justify her actions, wanting to make sure she had the attention of the elders before she descended, she was old enough that she could be honest with herself.

She'd been stalling.

Gan Ou hadn't set foot in her homeland since her banishment. Any Wind Person would have been in their right to kill her if she had.

Every spring, Gan Ou had gone to the border of the two lands, the demarcation growing sharper as time went on. Some years, it was pure torture to feel the soft winds blowing and trace the scents of the sweet lilies and daffodils blooming just over the line. Other years, it was a balm to her soul, smoothing away the rough stone edges that had crept in.

Gan Ou tried to prepare herself for the soft earth that greeted her as she transformed, her giant claws becoming bare feet. She couldn't help but give a soft cry as she felt the ground she recognized as *home* push up to sustain her. Strength flowed into her calves, knees, thighs, and beyond, as well as a warmth she hadn't realized was missing.

However, she couldn't wonder at that now, or revel in the smell of wood fires, the taste of fine cheese and sweet cider carried on the winds, the warm blanket feel of *home*.

She stood up straight and proud. Though clothes would

make her feel better, she had no shame being naked, showing her true form with her sagging breasts, pot belly, and scraggly arms.

Before Gan Ou could speak, one of the elders took two steps forward. "Gan Ou. You were banished. Why have you returned? Are you seeking an easy death?"

Gan Ou peered at the speaker, swallowing hard against a suddenly dry throat. It was Ru Jing, the boy she'd fought and killed over. He was an elder now?

"I carry disturbing news," Gan Ou said. "Otherwise I would never have returned. I know the consequences of my actions."

The three elders looked at each other. Gan Ou didn't know the names of the other two. Hopefully they at least would be willing to hear her.

One of the others took a step forward, a short, squat person wearing a plain brown sweater over loose black pants. "We will hear your news," she said loudly. "Then make our judgement."

Gan Ou bowed her head in acquiescence. She realized now that her hope had been foolish, that somehow her news might allay her banishment.

At least if the elders voted against her, she would have an easy death. And there was something to be said for that at her age.

THE ROOM the elders led Gan Ou into was warm and humid. A small fire burned in the center of the floor, the smoke magically directed up and out through the hole in the center of the round domed roof. The walls were covered in golden, polished maple, the boards smoothed together as if they actually stood in the center of a great tree.

The rest of the elders still sat in the room on long benches, their conversations stilling as Gan Ou entered the room. She wasn't sure if any of them recognized her, but she thought one or two might.

An attendant threw a wool blanket over Gan Ou's shoulders. She automatically tucked it over and around her, hiding her nakedness without being overly fussy about it.

The nine elders gathered on their long benches, all facing her. She stood to the side of the small fire in order to address them, taking a wider stance, her hands behind her back.

"The elk are missing," she said starkly.

"What?" Ru Jing asked. "What nonsense are you speaking?"

"The form of the elk has vanished from the world," Gan Ou said. "They've been taken."

"All of them?" the one female elder said, who'd come outside to see Gan Ou.

"All of them," Gan Ou said.

The elders stirred at this, as if a wind blew around them, carrying short snatches of conversation that Gan Ou couldn't quite make out.

One of the elders stood. He stripped off his green shirt, red trousers, and gray underclothes. He had the pot belly of an old person, though he also had broad shoulders and his arms were still muscular and strong. Naked, he did as Gan Ou had done four days before, and reached for the form of the elk.

His closed eyes popped open. He looked at the elders in alarm. Sweat broke out across his brow as he reached for the form again.

"They're gone," he said, his voice breaking as he spoke. "It's as if the form has never existed." He turned and glared at Gan Ou. "What did you do?"

She shrugged. She knew that her attitude was what had gotten her into trouble in the first place, but she couldn't help it. She'd been young and set in her ways, and now, that she was older, she was even more set. "I didn't do anything," she sneered. "A young person, Ka Lem, came with his teacher to the marketplace and challenged me to find the form of the elk."

"Where?" Ru Jing challenged.

"In Killapany," Gan Ou assured them. "I live there." She took a deep breath. The elders weren't her enemy. Not really. "Ka Lem told me that the elk were missing. I didn't believe him, same as you wouldn't. But I couldn't transform into an elk. Reaching for them is like reaching into an empty stone cave."

The elder who'd failed to find the elk form shivered and nodded. "Yes. Exactly." He picked up his clothes, seeming diminished, older than he'd first appeared.

"Someone had to inform you what had happened," Gan Ou told the elders. "I volunteered. That was four days ago." Four days of hard flying, of barely resting, of constantly hurrying on the winds to reach the capital of the Wind People.

"Where is Ka Lem?" asked the person.

"He went to tell the Sea People the news, as well as to see if they know anything," Gan Ou said. They hadn't said much to each other. "He'll return here soon," she added, though she didn't know that for certain.

"The news you bring is important," the elder said. She glanced at the other elders before she stood up. "I, Hi Lop, the eldest of the council of elders, temporarily allay your banishment."

Ru Jing looked as if he might object. Before he could say anything, Hi Lop continued. "You will have further chances to prove yourself, before we make the final decision about your banishment. Your first task will be to inform the other villages and collect what news you can."

Gan Ou wanted to object. Why should *she* do this? Didn't the elders have runners who could do this work better than an old person?

Then she realized the real reason why Hi Lop had given her this menial task. It wasn't something an old person should do, someone who should be respected, her place next to the fire guaranteed, her word always listened to.

However, if Gan Ou wanted her banishment reversed, she was going to have to do anything and everything that the elders asked her to do, to show that she really was interested in coming back home.

Gan Ou bowed her head to Hi Lop. "I understand," she said, attempting to sound grave and not as peevish as she felt. "I will travel as fast as any wind."

Hi Lop gave her a serene smile. "See that you do. And be careful," she instructed before she turned her back on Gan Ou, facing the rest of the elders.

Gan Ou recognized a dismissal when she saw one. Though it rankled to be dismissed so casually, she turned without a word or a caustic remark and walked out of the council room, into the front hallway. Then she paused, considering.

Where should she go first? What villages should she visit? How could she spread this word fastest among the Wind People? And why hadn't anyone discovered this before now?

The attendant who'd given Gan Ou the blanket walked forward. "Excuse me," she said quietly. "May I offer you food and drink before you start?"

"Thank you," Gan Ou said. She felt herself smiling, the action vaguely unfamiliar. She hadn't smiled a lot while she'd been with the Stone People. However, the Wind People had a sense of hospitality unequaled among the other Peoples, even though the Sea People claimed to be just as hospitable. But they never had relatives or strangers trotting up to their door, or falling out of the sky and landing in their yard, carrying nothing when they came to visit.

Sune Li had set forth strong rules when it came to giving aid to strangers, particularly ones who'd been traveling in a form other than that of a Wind Person. Too many tales told of the consequences of not being a gracious host when a stranger appeared at their door.

Gan Ou quickly ate the finely smoked ham served with still warm bread and soft cheese, along with a large serving of roasted turnips and parsnips, drinking down the sharp cider. She needed her strength if she was to travel up and down all the lands of the Wind People.

The attendant—Ban Ko—also brought Gan Ou a map so that she could pick a direction. Shan Yu, the capital, sat roughly in the center of the territory claimed by the Wind People when measured east and west. However, it was more north than south, maybe three-quarters of the way up from the southern-most tip.

Gan Ou chose to go east and south first. She would travel down along the Da Yan river, telling the Wind People who lived on the banks of the river, letting them spread the news along the waters and further east. Once she reached the southernmost part of the main market road, she'd turn around and come back toward Shan Yu, stopping at the capital again before traveling further north.

While she was gone, she hoped that the elders would discover something about the missing elk, what had happened to them.

As well as figure out how to stop it from happening to any other species.

"I THINK I know why no one had discovered the elk were missing before now," Ba Zing, Gan Ou's host for the evening, said.

"Really?" Gan Ou asked. "Why is that?"

They sat outside of Ba Zing's hut with half a dozen other elders from the local area. A huge bonfire kept those closest to the flames warm enough, despite the winter night cold settling in. At the village feast that night, they'd served Gan Ou a fish stew that she'd never had before, cooked with tomatoes, garlic, onions, potatoes, and dill. It contained many different types of fish from the Da Yan river, and was both fatty and sweet.

It had taken Gan Ou two days to reach the river and the first village. Then she'd traveled south for another two days, stopping at each village then continuing on. In the map she held in her mind, she was close to the halfway point of the Wind People's territory, equal distance from the southern and northern most tips, on the far eastern side.

Ba Zing nodded again before speaking. Gan Ou liked the elder and the care she put into her words. She was a deep thinker. Gan Ou was surprised that Ba Zing hadn't been tapped to be one of the primary elders and move to the capital. Or maybe she had been asked, and had turned the position down, so that she could stay in her home village with her children and grandchildren.

"Upon hearing your news, I tried to reach the elk form, as I'm sure others have done. I couldn't," Ban Zing said slowly. "Instead of continuing to strain, I held myself in readiness and meditated on the missing form. I finally came to realize that it never would have occurred to me to try to transform into an elk. Not now." She paused, obviously searching for the words. "When I try to think about the elk, my thoughts slide away, as if the image of the elk is covered in slippery oil. A deep part of my soul had already realized that the elk were missing. It's difficult to think about them, to think about transforming into the form. If you weren't holding yourself in awareness, you might not realize that you'd choose other forms to transform into without really thinking about it."

Gan Ou nodded. She had no idea if Ba Zing's assessment was correct, but it made as much sense as anything else, that the minds of the Wind People would shift away from the form of the elk without them realizing it. That would explain why no one had discovered the form was missing. Possibly no one else had the form as fixed in their mind, determined to take it, as Kan Li had.

"Where will you go in the morning?" another of the elders asked.

Gan Ou nodded to the person, unwilling to admit that she didn't remember his name. "I'll go east," she said grimly. "Toward the fires."

The elders had had news of their own for Gan Ou when she'd arrived: what seemed to be wildfires burned to the east. But that made no sense. It was winter, and the fall had been wet. Nothing should be burning, not at this time of year.

"Do you think it's wise to go toward the fires instead of traveling to the next village with your news?" Ba Zing asked.

"You'll send runners to Shan Yu as well, right? Telling them about the fires?" Gan Ou asked in return. The elders in the village had been debating telling anyone else about the news, not wanting to bother the elders in Shan Yu. However, due to the missing elk, they'd agreed to send a message to the capital. Anything unusual needed to be reported.

"The runners have already left," Ba Zing said. She paused, then added, "You must be careful on your journey. Just like the missing elk, the fires burning on the eastern horizon fill me with unease."

"I will be," Gan Ou promised. She'd only just come

home to the lands of the Wind People. If the elders decreed that she should die for doing so, she would accept their judgement without complaint. In the meanwhile, she would be extra cautious. She wasn't about to throw her life away on a whim, not when there was a chance she could come home to stay.

GAN OU SAT at the top of the tallest tree that would support her weight as a huge eagle and peered to the east. A gray smudge formed across the horizon. She didn't see flames, but she smelled traces of smoke on the wind. Not the comforting scent of hearth fires, but the sharp smell of a grass fire.

It had taken her two days to fly far enough east to see even the smoke. She was so grateful to Ba Zing for telling her. It was just luck that someone from Ba Zing's village had been out exploring, otherwise the Wind People might not have learned about the fires at all, not until they were much closer.

The smoke filled Gan Ou with unease, as Ba Zing had said. Gan Ou wasn't certain why, though she did feel, deep down in her bones, that a natural fire would never spook her so badly, even in the eagle form she currently wore.

Prairies and meadows spread out across the empty spaces beyond the woods Gan Ou sat in. There wouldn't be any true forests after this. There would be only copses of trees, scattered across wide open plain.

Did it make sense to remain as such a big bird? If there were no natural places for her to rest or stay? No forests for her to sleep in? The fires—if that was what was causing the smoke—were still at least a day away, though she couldn't say for certain, not given the haze that filled the air.

Bison were native to the prairies. As were certain types of oxen, sheep, and goats. She shied away from any of the deer forms, though they'd likely be fast. She finally decided to change into the shape of a large wolf. It would take a lot of mice, rabbits, and other small creatures to feed herself, but she'd still be able to move swiftly over the land.

Gan Ou fluttered down to the ground under the trees, the soft pine needles cushioning her feet, then made the transformation directly, without bothering to change into a Wind Person in between.

A great gray wolf with golden eyes stared out across the open space before it. She growled softly, a deep rumbling sound in her throat.

Though she could no longer see the smoke on the horizon, the smell was now sharper. Her wolf instincts told her to run the other direction, not into the danger ahead.

Gan Ou shook her head and persisted, putting first one paw, then the next, walking out from under the trees and onto the grasslands.

She promised herself that she didn't have to get that close to the fire, didn't have to breathe in too much smoke. She just had to see what was there to report to the elders before she could turn tail and flee.

Chapter Eight

STONE

NOALANON SIGHED WITH FRUSTRATION, standing in front of the city council. It had taken zir a lot of time to get the council to listen to zir.

Now, it felt to zir that they deliberately didn't want to understand zir message.

"What do you mean, the elk have gone missing?" Juhala asked. All of the seats on the council were elected, not hereditary. Juhala was Noalanon's local representative. Noalanon had spent a lot of time in zir office the past few days, wearing Juhala down until ze finally put Noalanon's name on the list of speakers for that week's meeting. Originally, the council hadn't wanted to grant Noalanon an audience, insisting that ze put zir name on a list and wait a month before they'd talk with zir.

Noalanon was the last to speak that night, and ze could tell the council members were both irritated and impatient.

"According to the Wind People, all of the elk are now gone," Noalanon said. When ze hadn't been haunting the office of zir local representative, ze had been going to every Wind Person ze knew, asking about the elk.

They all confirmed what Ka Lem had told zir. The elk no longer existed. It scared the Wind People deeply, filling them with an unease. Now, whenever Noalanon saw a group of three or more Wind People together, winds always seemed to circle around them, like a growing storm.

"How is it even possible for the elk to be missing?" Mahletik asked. Ze was the oldest council member, the representative of the wealthy mine owners who tended to live in the same northern quadrant of the city. Ze wore the finest shirt of all the council members, a rich black cotton that had been treated so it had a subtle sheen to it.

Noalanon shook zir head. Ze stood on the floor before the raised platform. A tall table made out of highly polished granite rose up before her, like a stone wall. The five council members sat behind it, guarded, cautious. Traditionally, each council member represented a different guild: miners, merchants, artisans, teachers, and builders. If someone wasn't a member of one of the guilds, ze representative was decided based on where ze lived in the city.

While Noalanon could appreciate the grays and blacks of the fine table, the marble mosaic in the shape of a five pointed star that she stood on, as well as the creamy, polished, white-marble walls shot through with gold, zir still wished that all of them were talking in a tavern someplace, sipping hot drinks and just conversing. The formality of the chamber irked zir, as well as the deliberate placement of the petitioner so far beneath the council.

"No one knows how the elk have gone missing. Who has taken them," Noalanon said. Ze didn't want to repeat Ka Lem's dream about a mysterious person who wore the bones of the elk and started to burn the world down, but ze would if ze had to. However, it was just a dream. Not a fact.

"Did the Wind People simply misplace them?" Juhala asked. "I mean, that would be typical of them."

"No, it would not be," Noalanon said, trying not to grind zir teeth while talking. "Yes, the Wind People are impetuous. I work with them every day." Ze paused, then continued. "I don't want to say that they worship all the animal forms that they can transform into." Noalanon ignored the snort of derision that came from one of the council members. "However, they do care about each and every form. They wouldn't just *lose* one of the species. Something—or someone—took them. Killed them all."

"Could it have been caused by some sort of plague created by the Sea People?" Mahletik asked.

"Why would the Sea People do such a thing?" Noalanon said, surprised. Besides, it was just a myth that the Sea People could create plagues, right? Ze'd never met a Sea Person who admitted to such an ability. Plagues frequently wiped out portions of the Sea People's population because they didn't have a strong constitution. Not because their own people created them. Right?

"The Sea People wouldn't have done it on purpose, no," Mahletik continued. "But they've made mistakes before."

"And wiped out an entire species?" Noalanon challenged.

"Well, no," Mahletik said. "But whole families, yes."

Noalanon blinked, surprised. Was that what had happened to the royal family so many years ago? She couldn't think about that now. "I still don't believe it was them." Ze sighed. "There is something else." Reluctantly, ze told the council about Ka Lem's dream of the new type of People, the one who wore the bones of creatures.

The council all grew completely still, sitting like statues behind their grand desk. Noalanon wasn't sure if ze should feel satisfied that they all appeared to finally take zir seriously, or terrified at how scared the council now seemed to be.

"A new People, eh?" asked Sugaoshi. Ze represented the

artisans, and was the youngest of the council members. "That doesn't bode well."

"What can we do about it, though?" said Kinrahsy, a buff, strong person who represented the builders. "This loss of the elk. It doesn't actually affect us, does it?"

Noalanon wasn't surprised that most of the other council members nodded at this statement. "It matters because we don't know if these other People will stop with just the elk. What species might they take next? The deer? The oxen? Rabbits or sheep?"

While the Stone People didn't raise animals for food, they did use the fur, wool, and leather of animals for their clothing.

Noalanon's comment caused the council members to shift uncomfortably. The death of the elk might affect them, yet. If only they could look past their own stone walls!

"I am waiting for Ka Lem to come back from the Sea People, to see what he's learned from them," Noalanon said. "I would like to speak to the council once he's returned."

"Granted," Mahletik said immediately, before any of the other members could deny zir. "In the meanwhile, we will start our own investigation. Sugaoshi, start a search of the archives. See if anyone can find a hint about a new People, a myth or legend, even a vague rumor."

"Thank you," Noalanon said, breathing a sigh of relief. The council finally appeared to be taking the threat seriously. For the first time in a few days, ze felt zirself start to relax.

"Oh, don't thank us yet," Mahletik continued with a sly chuckle. "You're going to continue to be the liaison between the Wind People, the Sea People, and the council. We will need to craft a message to go out to the others who share our city, to warn them, but not panic them. You will carry that message to them, as well as bring back to us any news that they might have."

Noalanon nodded. That really wasn't zir place. Surely there were messengers who would be better suited.

But ze understood why. The council didn't want to try to sift through hundreds of different voices and opinions. They wanted everything coming through a single viewpoint. Preferably someone they already knew, and possibly trusted.

Zir.

"I will do my best," Noalanon said after a moment.

"Come to my offices tomorrow to start the task," Juhala directed.

An expectant pause filled the council chambers.

"Is that all? Do you have other news?" Mahletik asked.

"Nothing," Noalanon said.

"Until tomorrow then."

Noalanon bowed zir head toward the council members, then left the chamber. Ze found zirself trembling after ze left the room, both in anger as well as fear, with a smattering of relief thrown in.

How arrogant the council members had all seemed! As if they were more important than the people they represented! And now, ze was to be a mere messenger!

Noalanon bit zir tongue and stalked out into the streets, heading toward zir comforting home.

Ze would do as the council asked. Would be their liaison. Until the crisis was over.

Then, who knew? Ze had never considered politics before. But now…

DESPITE THE COLD that came with the crisp winter air, Noalanon opened the windows to the front courtyard of their house every time ze was home, so ze would hear a bird's call immediately. Ze did spend a lot of time out of zir house, though. Zir position as a teacher had been covered by the others so that ze could act as the liaison with all the Wind and Sea People in the city.

Noalanon had, with Juhala's help, set up a series of meetings in the evenings, both to spread the word as well as gather news. No one had heard anything, no one had any inkling of the strange new People, or what had happened to the elk.

The Wind People had organized themselves and begun testing all the other forms. A group of them had taken one of the children's picture books that showed almost every animal alive and divided the forms up. Then, every morning, each person would spend time flitting from one form to the next in the group they'd been assigned, testing to make sure that no other creature had been taken.

Noalanon reported that work to Juhala, who seemed pleased with zir progress.

That morning, they met in Juhala's office. It wasn't as grand as the council member room. In fact, it reminded Noalanon of zir own office, cramped yet cozy, overstuffed bookcases lining the walls, papers and books covering the desk. A window looking out on a beautiful courtyard was directly behind Juhala's desk. Noalanon wondered how much time Juhala would spend looking out over the picturesque statues and walkways and how much time ze spent focused on the problems at hand. Noalanon suspected Juhala never looked outside, or when ze did, it wasn't with wonder or delight but with avarice and thoughts of how to acquire more property, more money, more respect.

Juhala wore a light brown shirt that morning that emphasized zir fine dark skin, the color of rich fertile earth. Ze had black hair that ze wore long, like Noalanon's, though Juhala wore zirs in a braid down zir back. Ze had pale gray eyes that to Noalanon always seemed to be squinting.

"Why hasn't there been a liaison with the Wind and Sea People before?" Noalanon asked as ze finished reporting about the meeting that evening.

"There really hasn't been the need for one," Juhala said after a moment. "The Sea People tend to police themselves. The constables take care of the Wind People when they get into fights. None of them have needed to regularly talk with the council." Ze paused, then gave Noalanon a brief smile. "Except to petition for more fountains to wash their feet in, or more trees in the parks." Ze rolled zir eyes at the thought of such requests.

Noalanon bit zir tongue. Maybe it was because ze worked with the Sea and Wind People regularly that ze didn't feel the need to denigrate them. Ze had grown up always associating with them, thinking of them as, well, people. Ze had been aware of the attitudes some of the Stone People had of the Wind and Sea People, but ze had never really had to work with someone so prejudiced before.

"I'll have the last meeting tonight," Noalanon told Juhala. "Then, I'm not sure."

Juhala nodded. "This Ka Lem should be returning soon, yes?"

Noalanon nodded. "Yes. I don't know what's been keeping him."

Juhala grimaced at the use of the male pronoun. Noalanon automatically slipped between the gendered and non-gendered pronouns, as that was part of zir job, working with the other People. The Wind People were gendered, and could transform into either gender easily. In addition, they didn't always stick with the gender they'd been born with, but instead, became the gender they were most comfortable with. The Sea People were also gendered, though not as easy going about it as the Wind People.

"I will let you know as soon as I hear from Ka Lem,"

Noalanon said, standing. Ze was certain that Juhala had other, *much* more important work to do than to actually listen to one of zir own people's reports. Like perhaps buffing their fingernails until they shone.

"Thank you," Juhala said. At least ze sounded sincere.

Noalanon walked out, feeling a little untethered. It was an unsettling feeling, particularly for one of the Stone People. Maybe ze should spend the rest of the afternoon at the teaching house, helping out. That way, ze would at least feel useful for a change.

A loud caw startled zir as ze stepped through the front door to zir house.

"Ka Lem?" ze asked, stepping back outside.

The same huge eagle ze had seen before dropped out of the sky, landing abruptly in zir front yard. The creature shook itself, transforming back into the Wind Person Noalanon knew.

However, Ka Lem's eyes remained wild, the brown ringed with gold. He glanced this way and that, unable to settle. His hands were clenched into fists at his sides, as if he was prepared to fight.

Noalanon had seen this before, when a Wind Person has been too long in an animal form and was having difficulty remembering that they were a Wind Person.

"Come inside," Noalanon said gently. "I have food and drink." Ze had stocked up on Wind People food for when Ka Lem did return.

"Food?" Ka Lem asked, his voice harsh and screeching.

"Meat," Noalanon promised. "And hot cider."

None of the children had been thrilled by the idea of *food* being kept in the house instead of just minerals. They were all afraid that their friends would tease them about it. Jolapen had accepted it with better grace, but just barely. Only the youngest had actually been curious about it, though even ze hadn't liked the smell of it.

"I will come," Ka Lem said, nodding, his eyes still wild around the edges.

Once Noalanon got a blanket over Ka Lem's shoulders, he seemed to settle down more. Noalanon sat him at the back of the family's eating nook, placing the cold meat—ze thought it was a type of pig—in front of him and backing away slowly as he glared at zir, barring his teeth.

Ka Lem picked up the slice of meat with his hands, savagely tearing into it. Noalanon turned zir back, giving him some privacy. Ze poured the cider into a good stone cup and warmed the mug in zir hands. Ze wasn't sure what else to do until Ka Lem came back to himself.

When ze turned back, Ka Lem had finally picked up the knife and fork and was at least cutting the meat, though he was shoveling it so quickly into his mouth Noalanon had to bite zir tongue to stop zirself from telling him to slow down. His eyes blinked slowly at zir as ze approached. Ze placed the cup on the table and backed away.

"Thank you," Ka Lem said after he'd chewed and swallowed. "I…I rushed to get back."

Noalanon nodded. At least his voice was starting to sound more like a person's. "Eat, drink," ze said. "We'll talk afterward."

Ka Lem grimaced but followed zir advice. "Then I will need to fly to the elders," he said. "This afternoon."

"Couldn't one of the other Wind People go for you? So that you could rest a day first?" Noalanon asked.

"No," Ka Lem said immediately.

Noalanon couldn't help but smile at his affronted tone. How dare ze question such a serious young person and his serious task? "Are you sure?" ze asked anyway, knowing the answer.

Ka Lem quaffed down most of the cider in two long gulps, putting the cup down before replying. "What do you know of the Sea People's beliefs? How they think the People came to be?"

Noalanon blinked, surprised. "They believe there were People before us, right?"

"They do," Ka Lem said. "And they believe, or at least Liseth, the high priestess, believes that if any of the People—the Sea, Wind, or Stone People—go to war with the Bone People, we'll lose. It will be the will of the gods. The gods themselves will kill us all."

"What?" Noalanon said, unable to control zir surprise. "Wait. The Bone People?"

"That's the name that Liseth gave them. And it fits. People as white as bleached bone, who use bones to transform into other shapes." Ka Lem grimaced and lifted his cup back up, seeking the last swallow of sweet cider, as if to wash the bitterness from his mouth.

Noalanon took the hint and poured him more, warming it again before handing him the mug.

"I will have to tell Sugaoshi that name," Noalanon said. At Ka Lem's puzzled face, ze continued. "The council directed Sugaoshi, one of the council members, to search all the archives for a myth, hint, or whisper of another People out there."

"Good," Ka Lem said, nodding. "I'm sure my elders are doing the same." He sighed. "I haven't had any more dreams about the Bone People. Or the elk. Except—I keep smelling smoke when there isn't any there, when no fire is nearby." He shivered. "The flames. They haunt my dreams and make me uneasy."

Noalanon didn't know what to say in reply. The Stone People rarely had any use for fire, except in their oil lamps or their crafts. They used heated stones to keep their rooms and their houses warm, as well as just warming themselves when they needed to.

"So what do I need to tell the council about the Sea People?" Noalanon asked, finally daring to sit down beside Ka Lem.

He gave zir a very warm smile, as if he appreciated zir company. "Were you aware that the Sea People can look out of the eyes of fish and other creatures in the water?" he asked.

Noalanon felt zir eyebrows shoot to the top of zir forehead in surprise. "No!" ze said. Then ze paused. "There is an old myth that the Stone People have about a hero placing stones at the border of zir lands and being able to see out of them. Not just any rocks, but ones that ze had woken. The rocks worked as guards, telling zir when a person crossed into their lands."

Ka Lem nodded. "The Wind People have a similar myth, of a hero being able to talk with the birds, see what they've seen. But the Sea People actually have this ability. Not all of them, but some of them. So they've been crossing the land, skipping across the minds of the water creatures, traveling east, seeking out the home waters of the Bone People."

Noalanon couldn't help the shiver that crossed zir shoulders.

"What is it?" Ka Lem asked, looking worried.

"Something one of the council members said," Noalanon replied, "about the Sea People being able to cause plagues."

Ka Lem grew very still. "Do you think they can?" he said, his eyes growing wide.

"I don't know," Noalanon said. "I don't know if they actually have that ability or if it's just a story."

Ka Lem sighed. "I'm afraid that too many stories are going to be proven true in the coming days."

"What do you mean?" Noalanon said.

"The Sea People believe that this age, the third age of the People, will end in fire. And that's all they see to the east of the lands of the Wind People. Great fires and smoke burning across the plains." He paused, then added, "While grass fires are known, it's winter time. Any fires should have burned out by now. As soon as the Sea People reported that, I decided it was time to fly home and warn the elders. Before the Sea People actually found the home waters of the Bone People."

"Don't you think your elders already know about the fires?" Noalanon said.

"Though the Sea People can't judge distances precisely, not when they're traveling through aquifers and rivers as they do, they believe that the fires are several days' journey east of the border of the Wind People's land," Ka Lem said. "No one might have spotted the fires yet, though the smell of the smoke may have traveled that far."

"Do the Sea People plan on traveling to the lands of the Bone People? Once they discover it?" Noalanon asked after a moment, trying to piece together all that ze had learned. "Can they?"

"They want to negotiate with the Bone People," Ka Lem said.

Noalanon marveled at the amount of disgust he managed to carry in those few words. "And you think that isn't possible?"

"The Bone People have killed all the elk. What is to stop them from killing another species?" Ka Lem asked. "What do we have to offer them?"

"I don't know," ze said. Ze told him about the Wind People becoming most of the other forms of animals on a daily basis, just to make sure that no other creature had been taken.

"Good!" Ka Lem said, nodding. "I hadn't thought of doing that."

"This is why we need each other," Noalanon said gently. "Because no one person can think of everything, do everything." Ze knew that went against the nature of the Wind People, who were very individualistic, while both the Stone People and the Sea People tended to be more cooperative.

"The Sea People will try to stop us from going to war with the Bone People," Ka Lem said after another moment. "Even if the Bone People declare war on us, the Wind People. The Sea People are convinced that all the Peoples will lose any war. That it will be the will of the gods to wipe the world clean and start again."

Noalanon nodded but didn't reply. Ze knew that it would be difficult to get zir own people involved. If the Bone People only took a few animals, and burned the grasslands, what difference would that make to the Stone People? They could stay on their mountains, isolated but unafraid.

Ka Lem finished his meat and cider, refusing more when Noalanon offered. "I need to be off," he said, though he stayed seated.

"Rest first," Noalanon said.

Ka Lem shook his head, then yawned so widely Noalanon thought he might split his face in two.

"You need to rest," Noalanon said.

"I'll rest when I'm dead," Ka Lem said, repeating what he'd said earlier. He forced himself to stand, then kind of listed to one side.

"You won't be able to get far, not without taking more of a break first," Noalanon said firmly. "You are coming with me. You are going to nap. I'm not going to hear any more of your nonsense."

Ka Lem gave zir a slow smile. "Yes, *Mana*," he said.

"That's right," Noalanon said, keeping zir voice strict. "I'll wake you in an hour," ze added after ze got Ka Lem stretched out on the living room couch, wrapped in two more blankets.

Ka Lem's eyes were already closed, his breathing starting to even out. Noalanon paused for a moment, then indulged zirself by reaching out and brushing zir fingers through his soft curls.

"Sleep," ze said. "Rest. You have done good work. There is honor in taking care of yourself before you continue with your mighty labors."

Ka Lem appeared to snuggle more firmly against the warm couch cushions. Noalanon left him there, going back to the kitchen and cleaning up after his meal.

Ze would have to go to the council, let them know what Ka Lem had told zir. Ze wasn't sure what the Sea People would do once they found the home waters of the Bone People. Could they start a plague there? Was that why they had so many diseases traveled through their own populations?

After an hour, Noalanon went back into the living room. The door to the backyard was open. Ze walked in just in time to see a mighty eagle standing on the paved walkway, then throwing itself up toward the sky.

Ze stepped outside to watch the bird, losing it quickly in the gray sky. Cold winds blew around zir.

Was that the smell of smoke carried on the wind? Or was ze just imagining it? Paranoid?

Shivering, ze walked back inside, closing the door firmly.

The Stone People were known to be practical. Generally, they considered themselves the most practical of all the Peoples. Noalanon was perhaps less fanciful, less imaginative, than most.

However, Noalanon would swear ze felt something

different, something deep in the earth, pushing up against the soles of zir feet.

Something was coming. Change, or war, or perhaps something even worse.

Could ze do anything to stop it? Could anyone?

Chapter Nine

SEA

LISETH WALKED out along the main stone pier early in the morning, the day after Ka Lem had left. The land city of Shiboleth sat at the northern tip of a natural, curved harbor. The harbor itself was calm, the waters more shallow. However, just past the edge of the curve, the land shelf ended and the waters grew abruptly deep. The water city of Sillboden was built just past that edge, directly west of the land city.

The Sea People had several piers that they used as their starting point to travel between the twin cities. One pier, south of Shiboleth, actually had slides built into it for children to play on. The main pier was built out of solid stone that was painted each year with a protective coating, so the water wouldn't eat away at it. It was a creamy blue-white color that matched much of the building in the land city. Several stone arches lined the pier, with images of both sea and land creatures carved into them. During the high holy days in the spring, when the Sea People celebrated the birth of Ishkra, the arches would be decorated with beautiful garlands of seaweed as well as wreaths of fragrant flowers.

Only the very weak or the very old hired a stronger swimmer to pull them through the water between the two cities. Merchants, too, might hire one or two, though they had their own pier to the south that they generally used for carting goods between the two cities. The workers dallied at the edge of the pier, laughing and joking among themselves, not even bothering to hawk their abilities to Liseth.

Gray clouds covered the horizon, reaching down to the gray waters. The winds blew cold that morning. Seagulls called to her, begging for treats that she didn't have. She shivered in her plain sleeveless dress, though the Sea People didn't feel the cold as acutely as the other People did.

Liseth took one last deep breath, pressing her palms together and her hands before her chest, giving thanks to Ishkra, before she dove easily into the sea.

The shock of the cold water enveloped her, as though she had passed from a warm building out into a winter's day. It passed quickly as her body transformed. Her breath left her lungs, her gills opening up to take in the air she needed. Scales quickly covered her skin, warming her as they did so. Webbing grew between her fingers, and her feet elongated, transforming into flippers to help her swim. She blinked once, twice, and her eyes changed as well, growing as round as a fish's, the iris bleeding away until her eyes turned solid black. Though she couldn't feel it, she knew that the ridges along the top of her skull had grown more boney, and that her teeth had turned sharp and pointed.

Liseth easily swam through the clear waters toward the lighted city in front of her. Sillboden always filled her heart with delight, though Liseth preferred the land city. Some of the Sea People were equally comfortable on either land or sea. They tended to be the merchants, who frequently traveled between the two. Other people would chose either one or the other city and never leave.

There were stories of Sea People who left the inhabited areas and lived out past the warmer waters of the sea, in the wilds of the ocean. Liseth had never met anyone who came in from the wilds. The stories always came from a friend of a friend of a friend, nothing that Liseth had ever been able to pin down.

The Sea People never walked when in the water, but rather, swam between places, flowing in and out of windows and doors. They never stood upright either, but floated, their legs flowing out behind them.

Sillboden had tall towers, much taller than the land city, all ringed with light. Glass globes holding tiny bits of magical light were tied to the various stories, around the windows, and so on. The lights were there to keep the larger sea predators away, though the city also employed guards who drove them off.

The city itself had been built in a series of rings, growing out from the central temple. It worried Liseth that though the outer circle of the city was still lit, all the rooms in those towers and buildings were empty.

Not as many of the Sea People were being born, certainly not fast enough to replace those who died. The Sea People needed to do something about the falling birthrates. Most couples now only had two or three children, not half a dozen, as they had in the old days. Even if the children died, couples wouldn't have more to replace them. Liseth wasn't sure what the temple could do to encourage people to give birth more often.

She didn't know if the coming of these new People, the Bone People, would help or hurt their birthrates.

Liseth swam along the upper parts of the city before plunging downward, making her way to the temple entrance on the ground level. While she could, of course, go directly to the office of Bayaseth, the head of the temple in the water city, it would be considered rude of her to do so, to not pay her respects to the goddess first.

The temple itself was solid stone, coated with the same protective paint that gave it a bluish-white tinge. Small, colorful fish darted this way and that, sharing the waters with the Sea People. Living coral formed a decorative path, leading from the "street" out in front of the temple to the door.

The door to the temple didn't reach all the way to the ground, of course. Instead, it consisted of a wide, circular opening a few feet off the floor of the sea. Scarlet tiles circled the doorway, a dark contrast to the rest of the building.

Liseth easily flowed through the center of the temple door, nodding to the attendants who floated just inside, then glided down the aisle of the sanctuary toward the statue of Ishkra. Instead of seats or pews, long bars had been set up in rows so that the Sea People would have something to hold onto while they listened to a sermon or sang hymns.

The statue at the main temple in the water city looked very similar to the statue on the land city. It was easily as tall, twenty-five feet, and carved out of white soapstone with a granite core. The left, sea-based form of the statue had more scales than the land version, while the right side of the statue seemed smaller, diminished. Liseth knew it was just a trick of the sculptor who had carved the statue, to give it that appearance, that the statue wasn't unbalanced.

Like the land version of the statue, Ishkra had a smile on her face, looking down kindly at those gathered at her feet. Liseth always believed this version of the statue had a sharper smile, one not filled with delight but also with a sense of superiority. She knew she was just making things up, as the second People that Ishkra had birthed had only been able to live in the waters and that hadn't ended well for them.

Liseth held onto the rail at the front of the sanctuary,

bowed her head, and prayed to her goddess, prayed that she was making the right decision, prayed for the future of her people, prayed as never before that the Sea People would remain humble, at peace, and that they wouldn't bring about the end of the third age.

Finally finished paying her respects, Liseth turned to go. She was surprised to find Bayaseth floating behind her.

The two priestesses looked more similar in their sea forms than in their land forms. They had the same eyes in their sea form, both uniformly black, while in their land forms Liseth's were more green and Bayaseth's more golden. Their faces had similar structures, both with a petite nose, bow-shaped pink lips, sharp cheekbones and tiny ears. They both wore longer dresses that fit their bodies well and showed that they were both small-breasted though with ample hips. Liseth's was a pretty green color, that when dry, had a shimmer to it, while Bayaseth's was a dark blue.

Liseth clicked her tongue in greeting. "Hello, sister," she said. The tone of her voice was much higher in her sea form than in her land form, so that the words passed more easily through the water.

"Hello, sister," Bayaseth said. They weren't really sisters, but as they held similar positions—Liseth in charge of the main temple in the land city, while Bayaseth was in charge of the main temple in the sea city—they referred to each other as siblings. Others did the same, such as the land and sea regents.

Though Liseth hadn't come down to the sea temple before now, she'd made certain that Bayaseth had been informed of all that was going on, of everything that Ka Lem had told her, what her own people, searching the waters, had discovered.

"Do you bring any important news?" Bayaseth asked.

Liseth blinked, surprised. "I don't have a lot to add to the latest report, no," she admitted. "I just wanted to come and discuss things with you." It had only seemed polite to do so.

"Then let us go first have some tea," Bayaseth said, reaching out her hand.

"All right," Liseth said, confused. Why was her counterpart suggesting this? What did she really have in mind?

Bayaseth and Liseth swam out of the temple, holding hands. No one would think anything of such a gesture. The Sea People, particularly in their water form, often held hands as they swam together. It was an easy way for them to stay close as they made their way through the water. Boys held hands with boys, girls with girls, for most of their lives. There would be an awkward time in their late teens when mixed couples would only hold hands with someone they were interested in, romantically. Eventually, the teens would grow out of that and stop worrying who they held hands with or didn't.

Bayaseth led the pair of them to the small marketplace closest to the temple. The main marketplace was located in the northeast section of the city, in the area that was closest to the land city.

A teashop to the right of the entrance to the smaller marketplace was doing brisk business, serving glass globes filled with infused drinks, jaunty straws preventing any tea from leaking out.

Bayaseth purchased two globes, bringing one over to where Liseth waited. The tea wasn't as spicy as Liseth liked, but it was still good, the taste slightly bitter, like green tea, with hints of red seaweed and mint.

They floated casually with the other patrons, sipping their drinks, watching the Sea People come and go. Males with young ones squirming along behind them, carrying baskets for reeds and other goods. Old females who swam together slowly, talking seriously, like scholars. Even a group of teenaged school girls, clicking and giggling.

Liseth wasn't sure what she was supposed to make of the scene that Bayaseth seemed determined to watch. She kept her questions to herself, well aware that her sister wouldn't speak until she was damned good and ready.

Or was Bayaseth just making a point, making Liseth wait, as Bayaseth had had to wait for news about Ka Lem and the Bone People?

Liseth kept her sigh to herself, aware that such passive-aggressive behavior, while aggravating, was totally in character for the other priestess.

After they finished their drinks and returned their empty globes, Bayaseth tugged Liseth back to the main temple, finally going to her office.

Bayaseth's office was much grander than Liseth's. Beautiful pearls and precious stones were imbedded in the walls. A colorful mosaic of waves with turtles, flying fish, and other sea creatures covered the floor. Though the Sea People could keep books and scrolls dry using magic, Bayaseth merely had carved tablets standing on display on a shelf. They recorded a poem of Ishkra, welcoming the people to the sea.

Several standing poles were lined up against one wall. They were the equivalent of land chairs, so that Bayaseth could have several people meeting in her office at the same time.

The priestess pulled out a plain pole and put it in the center of the room, then swam to the beautiful gold and silver pole that was reserved for her use alone.

"So, what do you have to discuss this morning?" Bayaseth finally asked.

"Was there a reason why we went to the market this morning?" Liseth countered.

"I wanted you to spend some time with the common folk," Bayaseth said without hesitation. "For you to remember who we are, where we come from."

"Did you think I've forgotten?" Liseth asked, trying but failing to tamp down on her anger.

"Maybe," Bayaseth said, tilting her head from side to side. "We are the *Sea People*. Not the *people-who-live-on-land-and-sometimes-the-sea*. We come from Ishkra's waters, and will return there."

Liseth shook her head, confused. What was the point?

"These Bone People. They're a *land* people. What do we care?" Bayaseth asked.

"They are challenging the goddess," Liseth said. She was certain that she'd put that in more than one of her reports. "They will claim death for themselves. And the goddess will not only ensure that there is war, but that we *lose*. The third age will end."

Bayaseth shook her head. "That is one interpretation. Another might be that the Bone People are meant to rule the lands above the water, while we stay here, in the sea."

"The second age came to an end because the Sea People aren't meant to only be underwater," Liseth pointed out. Really, did Bayaseth believe they could retreat from this threat? They needed to confront these People. Not run away from them.

"We could still take our land form," Bayaseth said.

"Where?" Liseth asked pointedly. "If the Bone People rule all the lands?"

Bayaseth shrugged. "South," she said.

"And abandon our cities? Without a fight?"

"No, no," Bayaseth assured her. "First we try your way. You said you're searching for the home waters of the Bone People. Will you send a plague their way?"

Liseth grimaced. She'd never spoken that part of her plan

out loud. She'd certainly never committed it to writing. And it sounded so ugly coming from Bayaseth. Liseth would never undertake such a thing as casually as Bayaseth appeared to consider it.

"I don't know," Liseth admitted finally after a few moments of silence. "I may. Plagues are tricky, though, and are as likely to fell the creator and those around her. We need to find out what the Bone People want, first. We know nothing about them, their gods or their myths."

Bayaseth was silent for a few moments. "I understand," she said finally. "And I agree. First, we find the Bone People. See what they want. Learn as much as we can about them. Try to negotiate before the Wind People drag us all into a war." She paused, then added, "*But*. If that doesn't work. If we can't negotiate, and a plague is deemed too risky, we run."

"I don't agree with that," Liseth said. Running away would *not* solve the problem. Couldn't Bayaseth see that?

"Too bad," Bayaseth said. "If you want my support in your plan, you'll need to support mine. I will give you all the resources you need, including the best plague worker I know."

Why did it not surprise Liseth that Bayaseth knew more than one of the Sea People who could bring disease and plague?

"But I will only support your plan if you will support mine," Bayaseth added. "And you need my help. More than you realize."

Liseth pressed her lips together to prevent herself from replying immediately. Did Bayaseth actually think that Liseth was that arrogant? That the Sea People who lived on the land would be able to solve this issue without the help of those who lived under the waters?

She didn't want to support this madness. It would split

the focus of the Sea People, when they all should be working together, on a single plan, to stop the Bone People.

But what Bayaseth said was true. Liseth couldn't do this on her own.

"I will agree to your plan," Liseth finally said after a few more moments of tense silence. "But we need to put all our resources toward fighting *first*. We can't be working on two different goals at the same time."

"Agreed," Bayaseth said smoothly. "Now, what else can I help my sister with?"

Liseth knew in her heart that Bayaseth lied. As soon as Liseth returned to Shiboleth, Bayaseth would put all her efforts into her contingency plans, sending out scouts to find the location for a new city. It would put an emphasis on the water form of the Sea People.

Was Bayaseth that greedy? That she needed all the attention and resources of the Sea People to be under her control?

Maybe. But there wasn't anything Liseth could do about that at this time.

For now, she just had to win.

Chapter Ten

WIND

GAN OU SLEPT FITFULLY, her paws twitching. She felt herself running and running from some creature she could never quite make out, who never let her pause. Her lungs burned with the constant smoke and her eyes stung. Hunger gnawed at her belly but she couldn't stop running.

She woke with a loud growl. The day had grown lighter. However, the smoke and haze were so thick it was difficult to judge how early or late it was. The sun appeared as a stark orange ball, burning coldly in the sky. It felt as though it sucked the life out of everything instead of carrying warmth and life.

When Gan Ou rose and shook herself, white flakes of ash fell from her fur. Her legs still felt tired, her muscles sore from the traveling she'd done the day before.

It turned out that the prairie fires were hidden behind a solid wall of smoke.

Or…something.

The day before, Gan Ou had taken the form of an eagle for a while, flying up as high as she could, trying to see beyond the wall, but the grayness rose up much higher than she'd expected. She couldn't see beyond it.

She couldn't smell anything but smoke, now. Her stomach grumbled in hunger, but her nose couldn't find any mice or other small creatures for her to eat. She wasn't sure there were any, actually, as the smoke might have chased them all away.

Gan Ou stood and faced the gray wall in front of her. It would take her less than an hour to reach it, she was sure. It flickered like a wall of fog, as though winds blew through it.

It wasn't natural. Something magical was keeping that wall so solid and uniform, stretching up so high.

Did she really have to go through it? To see what was on the other side? Or could she go back to the elders now? Have them send a group of brave hunters or explorers through the wall instead?

Gan Ou sighed. She knew in her heart that she was going to have to breach the wall. She still had to prove herself to the elders. If she didn't, they might well decide that she wasn't worthy of being allowed to live with the Wind People again.

Gan Ou whined as she paced back and forth, unwilling to move forward. The wolf instincts that controlled this form really wanted to run away.

She promised herself that she only had to stick her nose into the mist. She didn't have to go any further than that if it was just awful, though she knew that she should push all the way through and find out what was on the other side before she returned to the elders.

Finally, after also promising herself a good meal of the first rabbit she could find, she got her paws moving in the right direction and started trotting over the flat ground toward the wall.

COLD.

That was Gan Ou's first impression of the mist in the wall.

It wasn't composed of smoke, despite how her nose insisted that there was smoke all around her.

She couldn't see anything in the mist. Her hackles raised and a low growl rumbled in her chest. Her animal instincts insisted that other creatures were watching her, though she couldn't see, hear, or smell anything other than smoke.

While the Wind People had myths of heroes who cast powerful magic well beyond transforming into whatever shape they pleased, Gan Ou had never experienced it.

Despite that, Gan Ou *knew* that she stood in the middle of a magical wall. It was not natural. Constant cold winds ruffled her fur and crept along her skin. The smell of smoke lay on top of a different smell, like burnt sugar, that covered the back of her throat, a smell that she instinctively identified as magic.

Gan Ou shivered as she walked. She kept wanting to transform back into the shape of a Wind Person, but she knew that wouldn't be safe. The wolf form protected her from the wall, as it didn't recognize her as a serious threat.

If Gan Ou transformed into a Wind Person, would she be able to call up magic of her own? Perhaps a great wind to dispel the fog in the wall?

Something deep inside of her said that she might be able to. It was like discovering that one of her teeth was missing, a hole she'd never noticed before, an empty spot where magic might have been located. The space wasn't as cold or as frightening as the place where the elk had been, no, this was merely a space that was ready and waiting to be filled with knowledge.

Knowledge that Gan Ou didn't have, that possibly none of the Wind People had retained.

She walked slowly through the mist, belatedly counting her steps to measure how thick the wall was. The mist had turned the world gray, blinding her like thick fog. But her feet knew the earth. The Wind People always had a sense of the direction they traveled in, even without being able to see the sun or the two moons.

She continued due east, her count reaching one hundred steps, probably more like one hundred and fifty as she hadn't begun her count right away.

Passing through the far end of the mist was like walking through a doorway, from one room into another. She felt, rather than heard, a *pop* as she emerged.

Gan Ou paused on the far side of the wall and looked around cautiously. She gave herself a mighty shake, as if tossing the cold and mist from her fur.

The land on the other side looked normal. Dried grass tickled her paws. Haze still covered the sky, and the sun was still an orange ball. The smell of smoke hadn't lessened, but it hadn't increased, either. A copse of dark trees stood off in the distance.

Wait. Were those figures underneath the trees?

Before Gan Ou could take a step closer, a whizzing sound coming from her left made her instinctively drop to her belly.

An arrow flew over her now prone back. It would have gone straight into her neck if she hadn't moved as quickly as she had.

She'd been spotted by whoever guarded the wall.

There was no reason for her to stick around. Whoever it was that had raised the wall were hiding behind it, and hostile. That was enough information for the elders, though she did wish she could stay just a bit longer and get a closer look at whoever was under those trees.

She turned and fled, racing through the mist and magic.

It felt to her as though fingers formed in the smoke, combing through her fur at first, then grabbing chunks of it.

A line of fire raced across her side—a lucky arrow grazing her ribs. She abruptly changed direction, no longer going in a straight line but veering from side to side. More arrows whizzed by, missing her.

She yelped at the invisible hands that now roughly snatched out pieces of fur. It took all her control to not turn and snap at the invisible hands. Instead, she slightly elongated her legs, growing her shape larger so she could run more quickly.

Out of the gray and darkness. Into the light.

Just a little ways…

Gan Ou burst out of the mist wall, fleeing as if all the villains from all the myths were on her heels.

A hand made out of mist grabbed after her, pulling out yet another chunk of fur from her rear quarters.

Gan Ou kept going, adding the wolf's fear to her own, an unthinking terror that helped her run faster, her tongue hanging out of the side of her mouth as she panted, her sides heaving.

She couldn't judge how far away she'd managed to get before she finally had to slow down, her energy draining away. Instead of the earth supporting her, it felt as though it fought her very footsteps, the winds blowing against her.

Glancing over her shoulder, she gasped.

The wall had followed her, moving closer.

Could it keep pace with her? Damn it! She couldn't stop. She couldn't rest. At least not yet. She still took a moment to lick at the wound made by the arrow along her side. The blood tasted normal—a good sign. It might not have been poisoned.

Gan Ou threw herself into the form of a great eagle

again, though there weren't any trees or cliffs nearby. She had to make it back to the elders, to tell them how close the others were.

She gave a great cawing cry as she struggled to reach the skies. Her wings *hurt,* as did the rest of her body. The patches of fur that had been yanked out had transformed into large chunks of missing feathers.

Could she even fly?

It took a few awkward flaps to get the eagle's body to cooperate, to keep moving through the air. Her Wind Person's mind had to be more involved, pushing past the instincts that would send the bird to a safe place to rest.

Gan Ou didn't want to continue, but she must. She resented having to travel so quickly, or, quite frankly, even having been sent on this mission at all. She was old! This was a young person's job.

But she had to prove herself to the elders. Even if this last flight cost her everything she had and her heart burst from the strain of it. She had a responsibility to herself, if nothing else, to do everything she could so her banishment was allayed, even if the elders did it after her death.

A small rabbit appeared below her. Without thinking, Gan Ou dropped down, sudden death in her claws. The fresh meat and warm blood renewed her, though she knew that such a pause would give the mist wall more time to gain on her.

She flew off before she finished her meal, feeling as though cold foggy fingers already stirred her feathers, though when she looked, the wall was far behind her.

She'd outfly this damned wall, the magic of these other People. Get herself to the elders. Then, she'd insist on a long rest before continuing on. She'd proven herself already, damn it.

It was time for someone else to carry this news forward.

GAN OU BLINKED TIRED EYES. Every muscle along her wings ached. Her belly grumbled from being so empty. She hadn't managed more than a few mouthfuls of food in the past day. She had stopped along the way at a couple of Wind People villages, letting them know of the coming danger, before racing away again. They'd done their best to treat her wounds. She wasn't healed, not by a long shot.

Finally, though, the city of Shan Yu was spread beneath her. Gan Ou didn't bother circling or trying to draw attention to herself. The news she carried had to be spoken to the elders first.

Fortunately, it appeared that the elders had set a watch, someone who waved to her, signaling for her to land.

Gan Ou fell like a stone, barely slowing as she approached. She braked sharply, beating her wings hard so she didn't injure herself as she landed.

Her feet still twinged as she touched down, the earth not as soft as she'd like. She transformed immediately into her Wind Person form, though her arms wouldn't stay still by her sides but kept moving restlessly, as if trying to carry her. Great gouges had been taken from her skin, still raw and trickling blood, from where she'd escaped the wall. The arrow mark along her ribs burned like fire when she took too deep of a breath.

The attendant shoved a loaf of bread at her. "Eat," he commanded.

Gan Ou didn't try to break a piece of bread off, but instead, gnawed directly on the loaf like an animal. She was ashamed of her actions; however, she couldn't stop herself. The hunger was just too great.

After a few bites, she felt herself settling down, growing into her own skin again. She shook her head, taking a deep breath, filling her lungs, wincing at the pain. Only then did she notice that the attendant held a dark brown robe in his hands, waiting for her to request it.

"Thank you," Gan Ou said, stepping forward into the warm material. She gasped as it came to rest on her wounds.

"Do you need to see a healer?" the attendant asked.

"Afterward," Gan Ou said. "After I talk with the elders."

She was proud of her growing restraint, as she finally managed to tear off a few pieces and eat them using her fingers.

The attendant handed her a waiting mug of clear water that she drained, finally feeling like a person again.

"The elders await," the attendant said.

"Aye," Gan Ou said, shoving a few more pieces of bread into her mouth and swallowing. They would be waiting for her. And she had news for them.

It surprised Gan Ou that Ka Lem was there in the chamber with the elders. Evidently, he'd arrived just before she had and was finishing up his news when she came in.

Gan Ou knew that custom dictated that she should stand while she waited for Ka Lem to finish. However, she was too exhausted for such niceties. She slid down against the wall next to the door, her butt hitting the dirt floor hard.

At least the earth here supported her. Had it actually been draining her strength at the wall? Or had that been her imagination?

Ru Jing and a couple of the other elders glanced away from Ka Lem and glared at her. She kept her own expression bland and took a few more bites of bread.

"We have heard about the fires in the east," Hi Lop, the head of the council said as Ka Lem finished up.

Gan Ou spoke up. "I have more news about them. That is why I returned early."

She struggled to push herself up to standing. The attendant who'd first greeted her rushed over to help.

"She's been injured," he said over his shoulder to the elders. "Huge bites taken out of her shoulders, sides, and back."

Gan Ou wouldn't have bothered mentioning them until she'd reached that portion of her narrative. It didn't matter that she'd been injured. What mattered was that she'd gone to see the wall and now had news.

She shuffled over to where the elders sat on their benches. Ka Lem had been given a seat as well. He looked as exhausted as she felt, with great dark circles under his eyes. Though she didn't know him well, she could still tell that his skin had paled through exertion.

Gan Ou told the elders of her journey to the wall, the smell of the magic that coated the back of her throat, the mist and confusion, how she needed to keep to the ground under her feet or she might have gotten lost. She dredged up every memory she could, every thought she'd had. She even described how she should have been able to call up winds and blow the wall away if she'd had the knowledge.

The elders seemed dismayed that the wall was guarded, that she'd been shot at. She even drew back the side of the robe so they could see the arrow wound. Then she told of her escape, and how the wall had tried to grab onto her. She didn't bother showing the rest of her wounds. The attendant had already told them about her injuries. That was enough.

"I don't know what exactly is behind the wall," Gan Ou said at the end. "I thought I saw people under the copse of trees in the distance. I know I was shot at. My guess is that the wall is hiding an army, coming to attack us. We need to be prepared."

"Thank you," Hi Lop said. "Your news was greatly needed." She gave a curt nod.

Gan Ou knew she was being dismissed. But she wasn't finished yet. "I need to rest before I go and tell more villages the news," she said stubbornly. "And I need to see a healer."

Hi Lop blinked. "Of course. There's one waiting for you." She paused, then added, "We will discuss your banishment before you continue your journeys, as you have already done a lot to prove yourself."

Gan Ou suddenly found herself swaying on her feet. "Thank you," she said.

She wasn't sure how she found the strength to turn and walk away, her head still high. Stubbornness, probably. That had always been both her greatest weakness as well as her greatest strength. She walked out of the room where the elders met on her own two feet, though, and didn't bother falling over until she saw the waiting healer.

Chapter Eleven

STONE

SUGAOSHI LOVED COMING into zir office every morning. The southern facing window always brought in such lovely light. Sugaoshi had always been tempted to set up zir easel and paint there some morning, but had never found the time.

Ze did have several of zir paintings hanging on the walls already. Ze switched them out regularly. Zir current favorite had a primarily white background with huge red poppies done in abstract in the foreground. The color of the background appeared white in bright daylight, but in both the early morning and late afternoon light, it would transform to a gray-blue. The red would also change, going from bright-red to a darker maroon.

Sugaoshi used oil-based paint for zir artwork. Ze had experimented with the other style of painting that only the Stone People practiced—they called it mosaic painting—but ze'd never found it as creatively satisfying.

To do a mosaic painting, instead of using pure paint, the Stone People would add finely ground stone, rock, or minerals to the paint, giving the work texture as well as color.

They had a wide range of mosaic painting techniques, from painting with colored glue and then sprinkling the powdered rock onto it, to the other end, where they added the pulverized rock to the paint itself.

That morning, the winter sunlight seemed pale and wan, as if struggling to reach through the clouds. Sugaoshi warmed zir own body up a little, so ze would feel warm all day.

Ze had zir office set up differently than most. Instead of the desk being opposite the door, ze had it on the left side of the room, facing the wall that held most of zir paintings. The window stood across from the door, and Sugaoshi preferred being able to watch the sunlight shining through it all day. Ze'd had a friend come in and create the floor for zir, a beautiful abstract circling and swirling piece done out of highly polished stones, the colors going from stark white through all the various grays to dark black.

Sitting in the middle of Sugaoshi's desk was the ancient picture book of the Wind People that had been found in one of the archives. It had been delivered to zir late in the afternoon the day before, and ze had decided to leave it for the morning.

Of course, ze knew that the council demanded answers right away, particularly if ze had found anything. However, ze had also been stuck in zir office all day, having meeting after meeting, and hadn't been able to get out and walk in the fresh air. Ze had justified not looking at the book until the next morning to zirself by claiming that ze needed to look at the book with fresh eyes.

Honestly, though, ze had just wanted the day to be done.

The book was a children's book of the Wind People, and contained animal forms. It was perhaps a foot tall, two feet wide, and an inch thick. The smell of ancient, musty paper rose from it. The cover of the book was clearly hand-painted, the colors faded and browned. The work was technically precise, but not very inspiring. Maybe that was the point, though.

Sugaoshi carefully cleared off the files on the far side of zir desk so that ze could open up the book full and not have the cover resting on anything. The smell of mold rose up strongly, the first page dotted with brown spots.

Though there was a bookmark indicating the part of the book that had caught the archivist's eye, Sugaoshi still took zir time paging through the book. It started in the sea, with beautiful watercolor drawings of different types of whales, sharks, and other fish that lived in salt water. The name of each animal was spelled out and sounded out beside it.

After a couple pages of water creatures, the book showed those who moved from the water to the land, like tortoises and some sorts of lizards. Then came a number of birds, which surprised Sugaoshi, as ze was aware that Wind People generally didn't take the shape of a smaller bird.

The book passed the dunes and onto the grasslands. The bookmark was between two pages that showed a creature ze'd never heard of before—a horse. It looked like a skinny cow, or maybe a tall goat. It was difficult to judge the size of them. Horses came in a variety of colors, had a smooth fur coat, with a floppy mane that went down their necks, as well as a long tail.

Had horses existed at one point? Had they all died out as a species? Sugaoshi didn't want to have to call one of the Wind People to zir office. They were always so disruptive. But maybe ze could tell Noalanon about it, and then Noalanon could get a Wind Person to tell them the truth.

Sugaoshi continued paging through the book. After the grasslands came forests, and then the mountains.

However, the entire back portion of the book appeared to

be dedicated to made-up creatures, those who ze was familiar with from myths, such as the dragon and the phoenix.

Was the horse a made-up creature? Was the picture just out of place? Or had such a creature existed at one point?

Sugaoshi shivered, then determinedly warmed zirself just a bit more. The sunlight was a bit dimmer that day, as the days grew shorter and winter wound itself more tightly around them.

Or at least that was the explanation ze used for zir chills.

SUGAOSHI DID but didn't want to leave zir office to go and meet with Noalanon and this Wind Person. However, ze really didn't trust the book in the hands of an anonymous Wind Person either. Plus, it meant being able to go outside, even if the day was overcast and cold.

Sugaoshi carefully wrapped the book in a large piece of waxed leather. Ze often used it for protecting oil paintings when ze moved them from zir office to zir home. Then ze made zir way through the lovely city streets to Noalanon's home.

The house stood in the middle of a row of stone houses. A short rock wall separated the various yards from the sidewalk and street. While the sidewalks had many people on them, the streets only held a few carts with oxen, carrying good to the market just a few blocks away. The houses were out of muted stone, not very colorful or stylish. However, all the doors were properly rounded at the top, not cheap and square. Plus, the doors had all been painted different colors. Sugaoshi approved of that, as well as the pretty white-gravel path that led from the front wall to the door of Noalanon's house.

Noalanon opened the door before Sugaoshi had a chance

to knock on it. "Councilor," Noalanon said cheerfully. "Please, come in, and welcome to my home."

"Thank you," Sugaoshi said. Ze looked around curiously. The place was cluttered, of course. Noalanon was a teacher, if ze remembered correctly. Only artists like zir kept their houses spotless and wide open, with as few possessions as possible.

A separate eating nook had been carved out against the far wall, a round table with a round seating area behind it. The rest of the room looked like a play area. Sugaoshi belatedly remembered that Noalanon had children. Sugaoshi had never bothered. Ze didn't even have a partner. Zir artwork was really all ze needed.

Noalanon led Sugaoshi through the front room and into the living room. A Wind Person sat on the couch. He—she —sat on the couch wearing just a blanket thrown over her— his—shoulders.

Really, it was just so difficult to tell! Sugaoshi just didn't see the point of genders.

The Wind Person stood up and dipped zir head to Sugaoshi. Ze did the same as Noalanon went through the introductions. Ao Shur was zir name, which didn't give a hint about zir gender either.

"Ao Shur has volunteered to look at the ancient book you've found, and see if he can find the creature," Noalanon said.

Finally! A clue. "Thank you, Ao Shur," Sugaoshi said, unwrapping the book carefully and placing it on the low table in front of the couch.

Ao Shur opened the book and studied it intently. "This book is very old," he said after a few moments. "Where did you find it?"

"The Stone People have ancient archives and libraries," Sugaoshi said, allowing zir pride to color zir voice. "That way, we can easily go back and study our history if we need to." Not that many did. There was a reason why the archives and their contents were under the purview of the artisans and not the teachers.

"Fascinating," Ao Shur said. "Most of our history is told from one elder to the next. We have a few written history books, but not many." He looked up and gave Sugaoshi a grin. "Too difficult to keep. The Wind People don't value books, or possessions in general, as much as the other Peoples."

Sugaoshi kept a smile on zir face, though ze felt the deliberate sting of his comment. Ze honestly felt the same about a lot of the Stone People, particularly those who weren't artists.

"There's no date on the book," Noalanon said, looking over Ao Shur's shoulder. "Can you guess how old it is?"

Ao Shur shrugged. "I'm not an artist," he said. "But I would guess it's at least a century old."

Sugaoshi sat up straighter, surprised. "Really?" ze asked. "Why would you say that?"

"We don't teach the animal form progressions like this anymore," Ao Shur said. "Starting in the water and moving to the land. I would think that would be very confusing for a little one. You need to start with the familiar land forms first, with the sea forms last. Or at least, that's how our books are organized now."

"That makes sense," Sugaoshi had to admit. Honestly, ze hadn't even thought about this as a teaching tool, looking at it more as an artifact.

Ao Shur looked at a few more pages before he flipped to the pages with the horses. He gave a low whistle, looked at a couple of pages before the horses, then a couple of pages afterward.

"That's so strange," he finally said, his voice almost a

whisper. "I've never seen such a creature before or formed its shape. But I *know* it, somehow."

"So it's a real animal?" Sugaoshi clarified. "There are a bunch of imaginary creatures at the back of the book."

Ao Shur flipped the book open to the last section and nodded. "These aren't real," he said flatly. "They do *not* belong in a teaching book. This book is all wrong," he said firmly.

"Maybe it wasn't used for teaching? But created just for the Stone People?" Noalanon suggested.

"It has the feel of a teaching book, with all the animals and their names spelled out. But if it isn't a teaching book, I don't understand its purpose," Ao Shur said, giving the book a stern look, as if the contents would rearrange themselves into a more sensible manner.

Sugaoshi wasn't sure why that mattered to him so much. Didn't the Wind People just create art books sometimes? "All right," ze said after a moment. "But what about the horses?"

Ao Shur stared at the pictures. He closed his eyes and grew completely still.

Sugaoshi didn't know that a Wind Person could actually sit like a civilized person. How interesting!

"There's a hole where the horses were," he said after a moment. His eyes remained closed and drops of water had broken out across his brow—sweat, Sugaoshi believed they called it.

"Is it like the hole where the elk were?" Noalanon asked quietly.

He nodded. "Wait," he said after another long pause.

Suddenly, Ao Shur surged to his feet. He threw off the blanket he'd been wearing, showing his naked body.

Sugaoshi studied it. The placement of the male organs looked funny to zir, unnecessary. Ze preferred the complete smoothness of a Stone Person. And all those muscles! A

Stone Person didn't show zir strength like that, despite the fact that they were much, much stronger than any of the other Peoples.

The last time Sugaoshi had seen a naked Wind Person had been in school, a drawing class, when they'd had to draw not only a naked male person but a female too, as well as both genders of a naked sea person.

The form was alien, but compact. Ao Shur's skin was the color of brown mountain stone, near the top of the holy mountain, when the summer sun shone on it.

He quickly stepped to the side, away from the couch, giving himself more room.

Sugaoshi had seen a Wind Person transform before, the body itself changing and generally compacting down, the operation smooth and breathtaking.

This time, it was as if a fine cloud had gathered around the person's body, wisps hiding his change. Sugaoshi could still see it, but it felt obscured.

The fur grew first, thick and dark brown, spreading across his skin. His curly brown hair grew down his back, shaggy and unkept. Then his face elongated, the eyes spreading out to the sides of his head. Finally, his legs and arms changed, the knees bending backwards as the arms shot out and down.

With a final shake, the mist around him dissipated.

A strange looking creature appeared before them. It wasn't very tall, the head barely coming up to Sugaoshi's waist. It appeared much more solid than a goat, its legs more muscled. It wasn't a big as a cow or bison, though, not that she'd ever spent that much time on farms that raised such animals.

Ao Shur took a few steps forward, turned around and walked in a circle, as if trying out this form, getting accustomed to it.

Then, with a great shake, Ao Shur transformed back into a Wind Person.

"Was that a horse?" Noalanon asked.

Sugaoshi peered closely, fascinated. Had ze just seen a creature that was no longer known?

"No," Ao Shur said. "Yes, but no." He walked back to the picture book and pointed to a much smaller horse up on the left hand side. "It's full grown, but it's called a pony," he said, sounding out the word. "It's a slightly different species. Different enough that it survived."

"Where is it?" Sugaoshi asked. "We've never seen it. Does it live north of here? South?"

Ao Shur shook his head. "It lives very far away. So far away I can't even imagine the distance. Years of travel away."

Sugaoshi couldn't help but shiver at the implications. All the People knew that there were undiscovered lands to the east. How far did they stretch?

"We need to tell the council of this," Noalanon said. "Explain that there was another creature who's been lost."

"Not lost," Ao Shur said firmly. "Taken. The spot where they were…it chills me. It's as bad, if not worse, than the place where the elk were."

"Do you think the same people took them? The Bone People?" Sugaoshi asked.

"It feels the same," Ao Shur said. He pressed his lips together firmly. "Can I take this book with me? Back to the elders?"

Sugaoshi knew that ze had to allow this. "I need to show it to my council first," ze said after a moment. "Tomorrow, you may take it. But you must return it." Ze knew how careless the Wind People were with all their possessions.

"I will. Thank you," Ao Shur said. He stood again, restless.

So like one of the Wind People! Never able to stop and

think, but leaping into action without a plan. Ze was suddenly very glad that ze was making him wait. Maybe he'd actually reflect on what was lost, maybe find something else.

Still, it worried zir that they'd lost not just the elk, but horses as well.

What else would these Bone People steal before they were stopped?

Chapter Twelve

SEA

BAYASETH FLOATED in her office after Liseth had left. Bayaseth loved the formality of the space, the beautiful stones and pearls encrusted in the walls, the stunning mosaic on the floor. She didn't have as many books or scrolls as Liseth had —she didn't feel that she needed them. She could remember everything she needed to on her own.

The Sea People didn't have as many books or writing in the water capital as they had in the land capital. So important people had scribes—specially trained individuals who would remember everything they'd been told and be able to repeat it back verbatim. Though all the Sea People had good memories, better than the Wind or Stone People, those of the Sea People who stayed in their water form tended to have even better ones.

Bayaseth had told Liseth that she'd get her full support; however, Bayaseth was still planning on splitting her resources.

It was finally time to put her grand plan into place.

Over the years, Bayaseth had sent Sea People down the coast to explore, to where the great river Lossheen poured out from the land into the water. The land dropped off sharply just past the bay. It would be the perfect place to build a second capital.

The land city wouldn't be as easy to build. That was partly why Bayaseth had chosen that location. Those who foolishly decided to stay in their land form would struggle more than those who stayed in their sea form.

It was time for the tide to change. For the sea form to ascend and be more important once again.

Of course, these coming People, these Bone People, worried Bayaseth. However, she was also certain that the Wind and Stone People could stop them, or that one of the plagues of the Sea People would wipe them out. Even if the Bone People kept rolling across the continent, it would take decades before they reached the sea.

And by that point, the twin capitals would have been moved.

Bayaseth didn't believe that the Bone People were challenging the gods. They'd killed off a land species. There were plenty more where they'd come from. It would take a long time before these Bone People would be a threat to the Sea People. If ever.

Finally, the scribe Calamish came swimming into Bayaseth's office. He wore a long gray tunic that had a simple belt around the waist and flowed to his knees. Underneath that, he had on a pair of black shorts that adequately covered his private parts, going down to midthigh. His eyes were set closer together, showing his great intelligence. The crest along his skull was also more prominent. His skin was colored a pale blue-gray, the color that most of the male members of the Sea People tended to be, while the females were more of a whitish blue.

"You wish to remember something?" Calamish said, reaching out for the pole that Liseth had been using earlier.

"Or do you wish to speak?" Calamish had been Bayaseth's personal scribe for many years. He had never shared her secrets or forgot his place and attempted to make suggestions.

"I will speak," Bayaseth said.

"Then I will remember," Calamish said, settling himself in for his task.

"First list. Contact Jolash about establishing a base at Lossheen. She will know the people who are most willing to move. Contact Kelimerys about establishing trade routes up and down the coast. Contact Pineeseth about providing building supplies." Then she continued, rattling off half a dozen more names, each with roles to play.

When Bayaseth finished, she paused. Calamish merely nodded, indicating that he was ready to go on.

"Next list. Contact Brodalesh, tell her to get her people ready. Provide anything that she asks for. Prepare the space they need for isolation."

Again, Calamish merely nodded. This was why he was her personal scribe. Because he never reacted to anything she told him.

Calamish surely understood the importance of Brodalesh going into isolation. It meant that she was going to start preparing a new plague.

While Bayaseth was going to go ahead with her plans of setting up a second water capital, it didn't mean she wouldn't support Liseth. If these Bone People could be killed off at the start, all the better.

It would just further her arguments, however, when some strain of the plague also broke out among the dwellers of Sillboden. They needed to not put all their eggs in one nest. The Sea People used to inhabit cities and towns all up and down the coast. They must do so again.

More space would increase the birthrates. Bayaseth was

certain of it. People would start having more children when they had more space around them.

Bayaseth finally finished off her lists, having Calamish repeat them back to her verbatim. It was good practice for him, and it gave her the opportunity to make any changes or corrections. Calamish had been well-enough trained that he'd remember not only the original, but the corrected lists as well.

After Calamish left, Bayaseth considered her options. She really should start with the first list, and go and contact Jolash the explorer.

She didn't want to. Jolash always made her nervous, not a state that the head of Ishkra's main temple should ever be in. However, she needed the rough and tumble explorer.

It was equally important that Bayaseth and Jolash never be seen together. Listening to Liseth's careless talk, Bayaseth knew that she'd managed to keep her plans secret, that her land sister had no idea how far along Bayaseth was in her plans of splitting the sea capital.

So Bayaseth sent a message to Jolash, using a new messenger, one she'd never used before. Bayaseth gave her the innocuous task of sending a supply of fresh reeds to one of the sister temples, to the west. Bayaseth insisted that the messenger use the bright blue baskets to make her delivery.

Jolash's people would see the blue basket, and inform Jolash. Tomorrow, they'd both meet in the far western market.

And Bayaseth could finally take firm steps forward in creating her new city.

THE WESTERN MARKET wasn't as brightly lit as the main market, or even the one nearest the temple. Instead, it felt dingy, the lights either spaced further apart or just dimmer. Temple bells marked the times of day—midmorning prayers, midday meal, midafternoon prayers, evening meal, followed by evening prayers. The land temple bells rang more often, but in their sea form, people didn't feel a need to mark the hours.

The temple bells had just rung for the midday meal. Bayaseth had supposedly come to the western market because a messenger that morning had reported a new collection of fine pearls for sale at her favorite vender.

The midday meal bells "reminded" Bayaseth that she was hungry. She looked at the various stalls serving food, finally choosing the one that wasn't just a stall, but located in a permanent building.

Jolash always indicated the place they were to meet using blue, whether it be a building with a coating of fresh blue paint (applied magically), a new statue painted blue, or like today, blue ribbons tied festively to the doors of the establishment.

The doors opened as Bayaseth swam toward them, closing immediately behind her with a solid *thunk*, probably locked or barred.

Bayaseth didn't bother looking over her shoulder or trying to see those workers. They would be under a cloud. In their water form, the Sea People could call up a dark shape to obscure themselves.

Instead, Bayaseth bravely swam forward, into the main room of what appeared to be a tavern. Bottles and sea-gourds filled a shelf behind a long bar that ran the length of the room, to the left of the door. Given the green tinge to the water, she assumed the establishment was not one that she would generally frequent, the liquor they served both too cheap and harsh.

The bar itself had been formed out of square iron bars

covered with a protective paint that was already flicking off, showing patches of rust. The bars ran lengthwise and across the width of the bar, giving patrons a place to hang onto while they floated as well as a solid surface for them to set their drinks on.

As Bayaseth swam forward, she thought she scented the smell of fresh blood in the water.

"A fight," Jolash assured her, swimming out of the murky end of the bar and closer to Bayaseth. "Last night."

"Ah," Bayaseth said, glancing around, though not actually seeing any blood remaining in the water. Yes, this really was not someplace that she'd ever go to voluntarily.

Had that been why Jolash had chosen this tavern? To keep Bayaseth off balance?

Jolash wore more clothing than most of the Sea People. Instead of a proper sleeveless dress, like most females, she wore a white tunic, like a male, though hers was shorter and ended at her hips instead of mid-thigh. It also had sleeves on it that were tied around her wrists. Under that, she wore longer pants that closed tightly from her thighs to her calves.

Bayaseth had only seen Jolash roll up her sleeve once, and hadn't been able to control her gasp. Jolash's skin was covered in gashes, sores, and older scars. Bayaseth hadn't asked what had happened, but she assumed that Jolash's skin condition was caused by a plague or disease that hadn't actually killed her.

The visible parts of Jolash's skin were a lovely creamy blue-white. If she weren't so odd and brash, and the rest of her skin so polluted, she might have been considered beautiful.

Bayaseth reached out and grasped the bar with one hand, the cold steel feeling solid against her palm.

"So what can I do for my grand ladyship today?" Jolash said with a grin. Only she was allowed to say such things to

Bayaseth, as the priestess needed the explorer. At least for now.

"I need to start moving people down the coast. It's finally time to establish a homestead at the mouth of the Lossheen," Bayaseth said with pride. She watched with satisfaction as Jolash's eyes widened appreciably.

"Really, my lady?" Jolash said after a moment. "That's good news. Great news."

"I need you to start collecting people," Bayaseth said. "The founding mothers of the new city."

"They might not all be proper," Jolash warned with a sly grin.

"I understand," Bayaseth said. It would be difficult to get Sea People who Jolash would call "proper" to volunteer to go establish a new city, far from the existing capital. The people who Jolash could recruit would probably be single females, people who, like Jolash, bore signs of plague, or people who didn't have all the training and education that someone like Bayaeseth might have.

Bayaseth talked with Jolash for a bit more, setting up details, agreeing to provide a certain amount of gold and goods in exchange for the females (with their males and their children, or at least a few of them) to go form a settlement.

Though she tried to hide it, Bayaseth was certain that Jolash could sense her excitement. Her plans were at long last taking shape. The new city, an important sea capital, was finally being built. Her proper place in history was being set, her name to become one of those taught to all the children.

When Bayaseth left, she had dozens of more tasks that she had to take care of. She couldn't risk delegating any of them. They were not only too important, but it was also imperative that Liseth remain in the dark, that her land sister had no idea of how far along Bayaseth's plan had already progressed.

They were reaching that critical tipping point, where Liseth's approval would no longer be necessary, when Bayaseth's plan couldn't be abandoned. Particularly if there were already people in the far city. The new trade routes up and down the coast would have to be continued so that the new capitol wouldn't be abandoned.

Bayaseth couldn't wait to show Liseth her new city. Right before Bayaseth unleashed the disease that would wipe out half of the land capital, targeting those who stayed in their land form and never returned to their sea form. Those who survived would quickly discover that the only cure was to change to their sea form, and remain in it.

The water capital would have to move at that point. Sillboden wouldn't be large enough to contain all the refugees flowing into the water. And Bayaseth would be sure to welcome them all.

Chapter Thirteen

WIND

KA LEM TROTTED down the lane as a large goat, his steps growing faster as he drew closer to his childhood home. The maples, elms, birches, and other trees had all dropped their fall glory, littering the paths. Frost kissed the edges of the leaves, leaving fine white trails across them, like frozen spider webs. Pines and firs still held onto their dark greenery, the branches creaking in the cold wind. The smell of hearth fires and the thought of warm ale urged Ka Lem to go even faster.

He hadn't taken more than a day or so of rest in Shan Yu, though his tired body protested traveling again. However, he wanted to get home and visit with his parents and siblings first, before he joined the group of hunters and fighters who were going to brave the wall. It would take a few days for the elders to make plans and get everything organized, so he had the time.

The hut Ka Lem had grown up in looked much the same as it always had. It stood alone, apart from the other houses, though the closest neighbors were near enough to signal to if there was an emergency, maybe seventy feet away. A three-foot tall fence enclosed the yard, grown from severely pruned boxwood and sweet bushes.

Weathered brown shingles covered the rounded walls of the hut. It had a conical roof, also made out of wood but covered in heavy moss. The moss would destroy the wood after a few decades, but in the meanwhile, it provided good insulation. Windows had been cut into the walls, covered in glass that was held together with wood, not lead. Herbs and flowers overfilled the window boxes, his mother's pride and joy, all gone to seed until next year.

Chickens ignored Ka Lem as he opened the wooden gate, intent on their scratching at the dirt and the dried grass. They diligently patrolled between the stalks of broccoli, kale, dill, and other summer plants that had gone feral for the winter.

Ka Lem changed back into the form of a Wind Person when he reached the threshold. He knocked on the door out of politeness, then let himself in, as he was arriving midday and assumed that no one was home. The Wind People didn't lock their doors as a general rule, as they never knew when a traveler might stop by and require hospitality, whether they were home or not.

The scents of home washed over Ka Lem—the spicy smell of the stew from the night before, the warm oil that had been used to polish the wood floors, the musky scent of his father's great wool coat, hanging next to the door on a long row of wooden hooks.

Ka Lem's throat grew tight when he found that his old housecoat hung there as well. The Wind People generally kept coats or robes just inside their doors, so that they didn't have to go searching for clothing when they regained their Wind Person form.

The front entranceway was not very big, built that way on purpose. It was a subtle reminder to remain in person form, as a large animal would be uncomfortable in this closed in space. An oil lamp hung from the ceiling, surprisingly lit, gleaming warmly off the golden color of the wooden walls. Dir`ectly opposite the door was a tiny alcove with an altar dedicated to Sune Li. A very skinny candle remained lit there, with five acorns scattered around it, one for each member of the family. Open doorways led to the rest of the hut on both the right and the left.

Who else was home? Ka Lem's mother would be very angry if all of them had left the house with lit flames.

Before Ka Lem could call out, a brown whirlwind came racing into the entranceway from the right. Or at least that was what it felt like to Ka Lem before he found himself wrapped in a fierce hug from his little sister, Pu Kan.

Ka Lem put his own arms around her and held on tightly. She'd grown. It used to be that he'd have to bend his head to kiss her hair. Now, the top of her head was well past his chin. Her hair was merely wavy, not curly, which was unusual for a Wind Person. She had huge brown eyes that Ka Lem always thought took up most of her face, wide cheekbones and a flattened nose. Her skin was the color of fresh pine, very pale and young looking. She wore a sturdy gray robe made out of felted wool, something that Ka Lem hadn't seen before, maybe something she'd received when she'd turned eighteen earlier that year.

"Why didn't you tell us you were coming home?" Pu Kan said as she leaned back. "Are you here for the season? Are you going to continue your training here?"

Ka Lem sighed. He knew he owed it to his family, as well as the elders, to tell everyone about the elk and the Bone People. He only wished for a few more moments of normalcy before he had to disrupt their world.

"We can talk about that later. How about some food for your guest first?" he teased.

"Oh! Sorry!" Pu Kan said, alarmed. She should have offered her guest food and hospitality at the start, before asking for news. "I was just so excited to see you! Come on. Let's get some food in you."

She raced away to the right, leading Ka Lem to the kitchen and eating area.

The hut was divided roughly into four areas, kitchen/living area and Pu Kan's bedroom on the right, while Ka Lem's parents' bedroom and the room Ka Lem had shared with his brother (his youngest sibling) on the left. The core of the house was built around a series of fireplaces, a small one for each room, all feeding into a single smokestack. A small hallway circled around the very center.

As a rule, the Wind People spent more time outside than inside. While the front yard was dedicated to chickens, vegetables, and herbs, the backyard had tables and chairs, as well as open space for the kids to race around in. They didn't have the ability to warm themselves, unlike the Stone People, so beside the back door was a huge basket containing blankets and robes for use outdoors.

The kitchen/living area was the largest part of the house, as it was most used after the yards. Under the house was a root cellar, but it was only accessible from outside. Pu Kan grabbed a wooden bowl and uncovered a pot of soup that had been sitting on the wood-burning stove. "There's bread in the cupboard," she said, pointing with her chin over her shoulder.

Ka Lem considered teasing her about making a guest serve himself, but it actually felt good to get it. He wasn't merely a guest, but family here.

Wooden benches, long enough to hold three people on a side, were pulled up to a square wooden table at the back of the room. The table itself was smooth from years of use. It was one of the few possessions that his mother had brought from her childhood.

Ka Lem dug into the food while his sister poured him a large mug of cool water. "Thank you," he managed to say after he'd devoured half the bowl and felt as though he could breathe again.

"You were hungry," Pu Kan said. "There is more if you need it."

"Maybe," Ka Lem admitted as he ate a few more mouthfuls of the rich lamb stew with carrots, potatoes, onions, turnips, and white beans. As he finished off the first bowl, as well as a second, he told Pu Kan all he'd learned, from the missing elk to the Wind People living in Killapany who were making sure that every form still remained, to the fires in the east and the speculation that the Sea People might be able to cause plagues.

Pu Kan's brown eyes were huge in her pale face by the time he finished. "You're going to leave again, aren't you?" she said. "Go see that wall."

Ka Lem nodded. "I have to."

"No. No you do not," Pu Kan said firmly. "You've already done your duty. You discovered the elk were missing. You brought news of the Sea People and the Stone People to the elders. There isn't anything else you have to do."

"I can't let this go," Ka Lem said. "I don't want others to have to tell me what is going on. I want to learn about it myself."

Pu Kan shook her head. "Mom always said that you were too stubborn to get out of your own way."

"What does that mean?"

Pu Kan sighed. "You know that wall is dangerous," she said slowly, as if Ka Lem were a much younger sibling. "And these Bone People are as well. But you have to see it for yourself, try everything for yourself. You're more stubborn than anyone else I know." She paused, taking a deep breath, before considering. "We both looked up to you. Shur Jo and I."

Ka Lem nodded. He wanted to ask how his younger brother, Shur Jo was doing, but he'd needed to tell his sister everything first.

"However, we also saw how you wouldn't listen," Pu Kan said. "You always went along on your own, no matter what anyone said."

"That's not true," Ka Lem said. "I listened. All the time."

"Then went ahead and did whatever it was you'd decided to do in the first place."

Ka Lem shook his head. He didn't think that was true. He wasn't as stubborn as all that. He was just serious. Born with an old soul.

"When did you decide to transform into an elk?" Pu Kan said.

Ka Lem blinked with surprise. "Before I took my soul form, as the bear."

"See?" Pu Kan said. "We don't know when the elk disappeared. According to you, the Wind People just stopped using the form as it became difficult for us to think about. We let it slip away. Only you could have discovered that they were missing. Only you were that stubborn."

Ka Lem shook his head. He didn't think it was stubbornness that made him try the elk form.

"You'd made up your mind," Pu Kan said quietly. "And you were going to move ahead and do it, no matter what anyone else thought or said. Or even what you might feel about the elk."

"Oh," Ka Lem said. He still wasn't certain that his sister was right. She might be, though. He might have been the only one of his friends who had stuck with their first plan of the animals they'd take as their soul form. It was possible that the others he knew from his class would have chosen a different animal without thinking about it. He would have to ask.

"So you've heard my news," Ka Lem said after a few moments. "Tell me the news from the village. How your studies are going. What's new with the family."

Pu Kan gave him a look that was far older than her years. She complied, seeming to understand that he needed this touchstone, this base, this normal family time, before he could continue his quest to find out what had happened to the elk.

THERE WAS a part of Ka Lem that didn't want to leave his village. Not just because his body was still so tired from all the traveling he'd done, but his heart was sore, too. There just wasn't enough time to spend with his mom and dad, not enough hours to tease his younger sister and brother, not enough moments of pure comfort to soak in.

He didn't have a choice, though. He'd always been called an old soul, a serious young person, more serious than most. He still was. He had to finish the task at hand before he could go back to a normal life.

He wasn't a hunter, trained to track or fight. He wasn't a teacher yet either, trained to cherish and explain the world to those younger than he. He was just a Wind Person. No special ability. Except possibly his stubbornness, that had led him to discover the form of the elk was missing. None of his friends who had talked about taking the form before had actually done so. He'd been the only one who'd persevered.

A few of the hunters from the village had gathered with him in the cold morning light of the main village square, the open area where they'd hold feasts in the winter, parties in the summer, and religious ceremonies throughout the year. His parents had respected his request that he say goodbye to them at home, that they not see him off.

Pu Kan had told him in no uncertain terms that she would see him off, would collect his robe after he'd gone and take it back home. While Ka Lem knew that others could do that task, he wasn't about to try to talk her out of it.

She, too, it appeared, could be that stubborn.

Four others had gathered in the center square, three females and one male, all determined to do what they could to help stop the Bone People from taking another animal. The elders had tasked some of the people in the village to taking on all the animal forms, to make sure that one didn't suddenly go missing.

There hadn't been war among the Wind People for ages. Instead of fighting, they tended to just leave, find a new village to go live in. They had plenty of territory, as well as multiple ways to defend themselves. There wasn't much crime either, as the Wind People didn't care for possessions. When fights did break out, elders with calmer heads stepped in to defuse the situation.

This was different. This was getting ready to fight against something they couldn't see, a People they'd never encountered before. The elders had promised large supplies of bows, arrows, pikes, javelins, and all other weapons, if needed. The Wind People didn't tend to fight in Wind Person form, though. Generally, they chose animals who had natural weapons, as well as defenses, before they joined a fight.

Ka Lem stood with the others in the cold dawn. "We promise to do our best to stop these Bone People from taking another form," he announced as the elders of the village came shuffling to the front of the crowd saying goodbye.

"And we will supply you with whatever you need. You

only have to ask," said Yan Shur, the head of the five elders of the village. "We will establish fast messengers along the road, from the capital to the trading villages east of here."

Ka Lem nodded. That was what the primary elders had asked for.

He looked at his other companions. They all nodded at him, indicating that they were ready.

Ka Lem looked out over the heads of the crowd, seeking his sister. She gave him a watery smile, tears leaking from her eyes already.

He would miss her. Gods, he'd miss this village. All he'd ever wanted was to come home and teach.

Now, he wasn't sure when he'd be able to return, if ever.

He transformed into a huge eagle, and with a great caw, spread his wings and determinedly leaped for the sky.

He told himself he would come back as his tired wings found a constant pace, taking him steadily away from where his heart truly lay.

He would come back. If it was the last thing he did.

Chapter Fourteen

STONE

NOALANON STAYED in contact with all the groups of Wind People, the merchants, artisans, and travelers, making sure that they continued to form the different animals every day. Ze was afraid that they'd grow bored of the constant repetition and would stop.

It wasn't until the second week that zir fears proved grounded. Ni Slo complained, when ze went to see him, that he didn't see the use of the exercise.

"There are others who can do this better than I can," he said. They stood in his tiny workshop. While the Stone People primarily worked with rock, shaping it, sculpting it, and forming it, they didn't do a lot with clay or porcelain. There was still a demand for it, however, and Ni Slo was one of the Wind People artisans who filled that need.

Noalanon always had the impression that the walls and floor in Ni Slo's workspace were done in tones of yellow and light tan, despite the fact that shelves filled the entire area with colorfully glazed plates, vases, and bowls, waiting to go into the kiln outside. The far door was double the width of a normal door, so Ni Slo could use small, four-wheeled carts to move pieces in and out. A huge potter's wheel took up most of the right corner.

Ni Slo stood with his arms crossed over his chest and a belligerent look on his face. "It's taking too much of my time!" he complained. "I have work to do." He wore a smock covered in streaks of red and white clay that didn't do much to protect the brown shirt or gray pants he wore underneath. He had extremely curly black hair that looked more like fuzz. His skin was the color of aged cherry wood, dark with red tints, with expressive gray eyes, a large nose, and a mouth that was turned down most of the time. Noalanon had no idea how old he was. His expression always led zir to believe he was older, but he moved with the strength and grace of someone in his twenties.

"Taking the various animal forms is also important work," Noalanon pointed out. "We need to know if the Bone People have taken another animal."

"Why?" Ni Slo said. "We can't stop them from doing it, can we? So why should we care?"

Noalanon nodded. "We actually don't know if can stop them or not. What if by taking a form, you prevent them from being able to steal it?"

Ni Slo put his lips together. "There's a whole group of us doing this here in Killapany. I'm sure that the elders have people doing the exact same thing in Shan Yu. So why do you need *me* to do it as well?"

"What if they do discover that another form is missing?" Noalanon countered. "How long would it take for them to get us news of it here?"

"Days," Ni Slo admitted. "Maybe a week if they aren't really pushing." He sighed. "I'm just so tired of doing all the same forms, day after day!"

Noalanon thought for a moment. Ze hadn't heard that complaint from the others, but ze wouldn't be surprised if they felt the same way. "How about this. Instead of you doing the same set, you and the others agree that on each day, you'll do a different set?"

Ni Slo tilted his head to the side, his face serious. "So on the first day of the week, I'll do the first set, then on the second day, the second set? While the others start at different places, maybe doing the second set on the first day?"

"Exactly," Noalanon said.

Ni Slo nodded slowly. "I think that would work. For a little while, maybe a few weeks," he cautioned. "We aren't children. It's tiring to flit through the forms this way."

"Tiring how?" Noalanon asked. Ze'd never heard a Wind Person complaining that taking a form was anything other than fun.

Ni Slo thought for a moment. "We aren't taking a soul form, which takes time to achieve. We're racing through the forms so that we can get back to our day. It takes energy to do it. Energy we don't get back immediately." He shrugged. "I don't know how else to explain it."

"Interesting," Noalanon said. Ze was going to have to talk with the others, see if someone else could explain it better. It took no effort for a Stone Person to perform any of the magic that they could. Then again, ze'd never tried warming one cup after another. Perhaps ze would get tired after twenty or so cups.

"I will let you know what the others say," Ni Slo said.

"You might ask them to think about what the next phase is, so that we have a plan when this gets boring," Noalanon said in a teasing tone.

Ni Slo took zir seriously. "I will." He paused, then asked, "Have we had any news from Shan Yu?"

"Not yet," Noalanon said. "We should be hearing from a messenger any day now."

Ni Slo nodded. "Thank you," he said suddenly. His face broke into a soft smile.

"For what?" Noalanon said, confused.

"For listening to us. For working with us. For treating us like people," he said. "Some of the other Stone People aren't as considerate or polite."

"You're welcome," Noalanon said, nodding. Ze'd been isolated before, teaching with other Stone People who had the same attitudes that ze did about the Wind and the Sea People. Working with the council had certainly opened zir eyes to the prejudice that simmered just under the surface.

Stepping into the bright, cool morning, Noalanon adjusted zir core temperature immediately. Ze always forgot how warm the Wind People kept their homes and places of work. And it was cold that morning, the sky a clear blue and the sun bright, but not bringing any warmth.

Midwinter was approaching rapidly, the shortest day of the year. The Wind People would be having a large celebration, staying up all night and holding vigil for their god Sune Li and the return of the light.

The Stone People would have a minor celebration at that time, but the major festival for Kiproary wouldn't occur until midsummer, on the solstice. The Sea People celebrated Ishkra's birthday during the spring equinox (and it always struck Noalanon as odd for a goddess to have a birthday).

Ze walked slowly through the streets. Tomorrow, ze would visit a different Wind Person. In the meanwhile, it was time to go back to Juhala's office, see if there was any news.

UNLIKE THE WIND or Sea People, the Stone People didn't grow pale when shocked. Instead, they grew very, very still, until they became like long-standing rocks.

The entire council, along with all the others, remained motionless as the messenger Lin Zi recounted her tale of the wall of magic approaching from the east and the fires that they couldn't see but that they knew burned behind it.

The council members sat behind their high desk, looking down on the messenger. The rest of the audience stood at the back, against the polished white walls. The formality of the chamber still irked Noalanon, along with how high the council members positioned themselves above everyone else.

"Thank you," Mahletik said when the messenger finished her message. Though there wasn't a head of the council, ze often filled that role. "Let us know if you need anything." Ze wore a richly embroidered brown and gold vest, with squared off emeralds for buttons, over a white linen shirt, looking every bit as rich and prosperous as the miners ze represented.

Lin Zi grimaced. She'd flown long and hard to reach them, collapsing in front of the dormitories, under the trees. They'd gotten food into her quickly, as well as water, letting her rest for a few hours so that she had the strength to face the council.

"I have already told my message to another Wind Person, who has flown off to carry the news to the Sea People," she said. "We will need to set up regular messengers between our capitals," she added, glaring at the council.

Noalanon fought to keep a smooth expression on zir face. Ze had already asked the council for that. They hadn't thought it was necessary.

"We will start that process," Juhala said smoothly. Ze wore a somber black shirt with a high collar that night and looked very serious. As ze was the head of the teachers, maybe it would fall under zir purview. Then ze glanced over at Noalanon.

No, ze was going to assign the task to Noalanon.

After the messenger left, the council started their

deliberations. Noalanon was pleased that they let the audience remain, and weren't trying to make these decisions behind closed doors. There weren't many there, only a dozen or so interested people.

It did surprise zir when Sugaoshi was the one who suggested that they send people to the wall, to help stop whoever or whatever was behind it. "If we harden our skin enough, the arrows wouldn't hurt us," ze added. Ze wore a pretty white top that had bright red hand-painted flowers on it, the brightest spot among the councilors.

Noalanon had to think about that for a moment. Ze knew that the Stone People could harden their skin. Miners did it all the time when digging, as did other workers. It hadn't occurred to zir that it might be enough to shield them from arrows.

Yagakilly, the council member who represented the merchants, agreed. "We need to give the Wind People our full support." Ze was the second brightest spot on the council that day, in a soft golden shirt that shimmered in the light as ze moved. "And I can help with the messengers," ze added, glancing first at Juhala, then at Noalanon.

That made zir feel better, that other members of the council finally supported the messengers. Really, they should have set those up as soon as they learned of the missing elk!

But there was only so much Noalanon could do, and zir contact, Juhala, wasn't always the easiest to get to agree to anything.

"I disagree," Kinrahsy said. Zir shirt and vest were red, looking like shades of brick. "We need to build a wall of our own. Keep these strangers out."

Sugaoshi snorted in derision. "Right. Because a wall of our own is going to keep a magical wall of mist away."

Kinrahsy seemed oddly undeterred. "We could build it so that none could pass."

Noalanon blinked, surprised. What was ze talking about? How could they build a wall that no one could pass through?

Yagakilly spoke up. "And what about trade? You might not think much of the Wind or Sea People, however, they provide us with goods, clothing, and building materials, that we would sorely miss if we cut ourselves off from them."

Kinrahsy didn't reply, but merely set zir face in a stubborn expression, obviously not convinced.

Mahletik spoke up. "I also don't want to send our people into danger. Who knows what is on the other side of the wall? The Wind People speak of fire. What if they have magical fire that can burn stone?"

Noalanon suddenly found zirself motionless. Ka Lem had said something along those lines, that unfortunately they were going to discover for themselves the truth of all those myths. Then another thought occurred to zir, causing zir to go absolutely still.

Was the wall that Kinrahsy talked of also going to be "alive"? Made from stones that had been awakened somehow, to protect their borders?

"I disagree," Sugaoshi said. "We need to send people to stand beside the Wind People when they breach the wall."

"They've probably already gone ahead and done it," Kinrahsy said. "They wouldn't wait for reinforcements."

"They certainly wouldn't wait if they didn't even know that reinforcements were coming," Yagakilly pointed out.

"The Wind People didn't ask for our help," Kinrahsy replied.

"They wouldn't," Juhala said, sounding as if the words were being dragged from zir mouth. "They aren't like us. They work more as individuals than as groups."

Noalanon couldn't help but smile. Juhala *had* actually listened to zir! And ze had learned something about the Wind People in the process.

Maybe when all this was over Noalanon really would go into politics. Maybe petition for there to be a sixth council spot, one that permanently represented the other people.

Mahletik, seated in the center of the five council members, looked up and down at the others. "So we appear to have two in favor of sending Stone People to help the Wind People," ze said.

Sugaoshi and Yagakilly nodded.

"And two against," ze said, indicating zirself. Kinrahsy also gave a vigorous nod.

All eyes turned to Juhala, who appeared to suddenly realize zir predicament. Zir expression grew as solemn as zir black shirt.

"You have the tie-breaking vote," Mahletik said. "What say you? The council will do as you decide."

Juhala appeared to take a deep breath, considering zir options.

Noalanon had spent enough time with Juhala to know that ze was probably not thinking about the good of the Wind People, or the danger to the Stone People, but rather, only about zir own reputation, and what this decision would mean for zir.

After a few still moments, Juhala looked up. Zir eyes locked on Noalanon's. "I vote we send people," ze announced. "It will take them time to travel across the entirety of the Wind People's territory. The sooner we send them, the better."

"In the meanwhile," Mahletik inserted smoothly. "I think we should investigate what it would take to fortify our own borders." Ze sent a pointed look at Kinrahsy, who gave a curt nod.

The council began talking logistics and Noalanon followed zir own thoughts for a while.

What exactly were they planning on doing to the border?

And what did they consider the border? There wasn't exactly a line dividing the Stone People's territory from the others. And yet, ze did recall the Wind People talking about how they knew exactly where the lands changed. Though Noalanon had traveled to both Shan Yu and Shiboleth as part of zir training, it had been almost two decades ago. Ze didn't remember feeling as though the lands away from the mountains were that different, though ze had always felt uncomfortable away from the hills, on the flatlands or in the woods.

Ze was going to have to ask for more details about that, why the Wind People considered their land different from the Stone People. As well as go and ask the Sea People, to see if they felt a difference as well.

And while ze was at it, ze might also plant the idea that some of the Wind People might want to start doing regular tours of the border, in the forms of birds, to watch what was going on there…

Chapter Fifteen

SEA

LISETH LISTENED to Ajooless give her breathless report, about how she'd traced back the Bone People, past the wall and even past the burning lands.

They sat in Liseth's office. Liseth leaned back in her tall embroidered chair. While she liked being in her sea form, it always bothered her that she never really sat when she was in that form. She also knew, though, that some of the Sea People found sitting greatly uncomfortable, which was one of the reasons why those individuals remained in their water form most of the time.

Light filtered through gray clouds filled the windows overlooking the courtyard outside. It would rain again soon. Liseth always liked this time of the year, the constant rains refreshing her skin, keeping her feet clean. The cold didn't bother her much. While the Sea People couldn't warm themselves like the Stone People, they found a wider range of temperatures comfortable than the Wind People, who constantly complained about the cold and the wet during the winter, or the heat and the humidity in the summer.

"Are you sure you've found the home lands of the Bone

People?" Liseth asked. Her primary acolyte Sasuelana, who had the best fish sense of any of the people the temple employed, still hadn't found her way across the empty lands to the east of the Wind Peoples' territory.

"I am," Ajooless said proudly. "I traced the tiniest drops across the arid steppes, staying far underground in the aquifers. It wasn't easy, following trickles of water," she added, making a face.

"Can you show me?" Liseth said.

Ajooless's eyes grew big. "How do I do that?"

"It's another part of your training, that you haven't taken yet," Liseth said, nodding. "The sharing." She kept her sigh to herself.

The information Ajooless had would be useless until she could share it.

"I'm sending you back to the teaching temple," Liseth said. She gave a wide smile at the look of horror that crossed Ajooless's face. "No, not for good. And not to the children's area. But to the teaching temple that's here, part of the temple complex."

Ajooless breathed a huge sigh of relief.

Yes, Liseth was really going to have to get the girl to stop showing every emotion. When she became high priestess, she was going to have to play it more cool.

Liseth scribbled out a note and handed it to Ajooless. "Go find the main acolyte and show her this," Liseth instructed. "She'll get you to the right part of the temple. Hopefully it will only take you a few days to learn how to share what you've found. In the meanwhile, keep track of those waters, see what else you can spy."

The girl had been tracing the water only. She didn't know how to look through the eyes of the fish in the water. That was why it was imperative that she learn how to share the taste of those waters, so that others could follow.

Others who might have more skills. Possibly even plague skills.

———

LISETH HELD her tongue and didn't bother asking the messenger to repeat what he'd just told her about the mist wall that the Wind People were facing. They sat in her office, the room lit by glowing phosphorous magic that Liseth had put inside the glass balls hanging from the ceiling just for that purpose. Still, shadows filled the corners. The wind outside blew hard, whistling as though it carried doom.

When Ka Lem had arrived with the news about the elk, one of the first things that Liseth had set up was a series of fast runners who would travel from the border of the Stone People to Shiboleth quickly. That way, the Wind People didn't have to exhaust themselves flying from one capital to the other. She assumed that the Stone People would eventually get around to setting up their own trail of messengers from their capital toward their borders. Everyone knew that it was difficult to get them to move quickly.

Many of the runners along the messenger line of the Sea People were either young scribes or scribes in training, who would remember any message sent to them and be able to repeat it verbatim. Liseth supposed that the Stone People and their messengers would carry actual written messages. Really, they just needed to be taught to remember things.

The Wind Person who'd been flying their direction had been flagged down by one of the messengers. Instead of having to spend the next two nights resting, the messengers had run tirelessly from one outpost to the next, carrying the word.

Liseth wasn't sure who would have arrived at the capital first, the Wind Person flying or her own messengers. Possibly it would have been a tie, as while the messengers couldn't run as quickly as the Wind Person could fly, there were always fresh messengers to carry the word forward, through both day and night. Plus, not all of the path was on the land. The primary market road followed along a large river in places. The messengers would occasionally slide from land into water and travel even more quickly than they could running.

The message about the wall had been sent out directly from the capital of the Stone People, so the messenger had no idea what the Stone People thought about the news. Which meant that Liseth and the Sea People had to make their own decisions, without knowing what anyone else was doing.

After the messenger had left, Liseth stayed in her dim office, thinking.

Would the Stone People send aid to the Wind People? They might. They might not. They generally kept to themselves in their mountain ranges. While the Wind and the Sea People would settle in all three capitals, there were very few Stone People who left the mountains and lived permanently away from them.

Then again, they had to carry their own food with them, their supplies of minerals, as they were unable to process or digest the food of the other Peoples. While the Sea People preferred their own food, they could at least eat what the Wind People ate, and vice versa.

Should Liseth send reinforcements to the Wind People's territory? To help them stop a moving, magical wall of mist and whatever was behind it?

But their lands were so dry. Anyone Liseth sent would be miserable. In addition, the Wind People had hunters. The Sea People hunted in their water form, not in their land form. They had few weapons that were ever used out of water.

Liseth knew she should send someone, and not just

messengers with empty words. The Wind People needed to know that they were being supported by all the people.

Plus, if the Sea People sent aid, that could possibly shame the Stone People into action if they'd decided not to send anyone.

Liseth drew a deep breath, letting the decision settle down on her bare shoulders. She wasn't worried about making the regents see her point of view. If they decided to withhold aid, she could still send a group along as the head of Ishkra's temple.

Now, it was just a question of logistics. Did she ask for volunteers? How many should she take? Would she get enough?

Also—what would be the fastest route? Most of the roads went north, up to the capital of the Stone People, then back south again to the capital of the Wind People. On the one hand, it would be easier to travel along well-established routes. However, the most direct route would go straight across all the lands. Shiboleth was actually further south than either of the other two capitals. Plus, the wall had been discovered south of Shan Yu. While there were paths and trails going directly across the lands, there weren't as many roads with convenient market towns and inns. Her people would have to carry many of their supplies, as well as more gear with them.

Which route would be better? She just didn't know. And she didn't know who to ask. Bayaseth would be of no help. Liseth had already sent a messenger with the news to inform Bayaseth of the latest development.

At least Bayaseth hadn't objected too loudly to Liseth setting up the messenger system, though she had thought it was a waste of time and energy, that the Wind People could just fly to them when there was news. However, the regents had all supported Liseth and contributed to the system.

None of Bayaseth's people would travel overland to go aid the Wind People. They preferred their water form. Having to travel overland for a month or more in their land form would be torture for them. There was no need for Liseth to ask for volunteers from her sister priestess.

But how was Liseth going to recruit her own volunteers? How was she going to supply them? And which path should they take?

Liseth stretched her arms up above her head and then leaned to one side, then the other, stretching her back.

She needed to go bathe her feet. Then pray, and hope that Ishkra would give her clear guidance.

AFTER LISETH HAD BATHED her feet in the fountain in the center of the primary courtyard, instead of going back to her office and the small altar she kept there, she headed for the main sanctuary, to pray at the feet of the tall statue of the goddess.

She didn't expect her prayers to be answered. But hopefully, spending time breathing deeply and in meditation would bring her the answers she needed.

Despite the lateness of the evening, the main temple was still full of gentle light. The warm bluish tint to the glowing glass balls made the long sanctuary seem warmer. Shadows hid the tall vaulted ceiling, making the room smaller and more intimate. The brass rails running along the top of the back of every pew reflected back the light with their own warm glow.

Liseth thought she was alone until she reached the front pew. A quick glance told her that it was Sasuelana. Her old assistant had retired earlier that spring, just after Ishkra's birthday celebrations. She sat on the left side of the sanctuary, directly in front of the sea form of the goddess. Her beautiful blue-tinged skin seemed darker that night, though that might have just been the dim lights. She wore a light green sleeveless dress that made her look elegant.

After backing up a few pews, Liseth sat down on the other side of the aisle, closed her eyes, and was soon lost in her own prayers and meditations. No answers came. No sudden wave of water holding the words of the goddess splashed over her. No high-pitched clicking noises carrying wisdom tickled the back of her neck. But Liseth did feel calmer by the time she finished.

When she opened her eyes, she wasn't surprised to see Sasuelana waiting for her, seated quietly on the pew just in front of her.

"You seem troubled tonight," Sasuelana said. "Is there anything this humble servant can do to help?" giving her a timid smile.

Liseth wondered yet again just how reticent Sasuelana actually was, and how much of it was an act. The acolyte had insisted on retiring and leaving the temple, showing much more steel than she ever had when Liseth had asked her to stay.

While Ajooless's training had come along nicely, she was just a girl. Liseth missed the quiet competence of Sasuelana.

"You remember the news that came from the Wind People?" Liseth said. "Of the elk gone missing?"

Sasuelana's eye grew wider. "I do. My lady, it's horrible! What are we going to do?"

Liseth bit her lips together so she wouldn't reply immediately. This was the old Sasuelana, the one that Liseth had grown so familiar with. Liseth's first reaction would be to tell her old aide that everything was fine, to spontaneously come up with a plan to reassure the person.

After a few more moments, Liseth couldn't help but

chuckle. The laughter broke something loose inside of her, and she found herself continuing to laugh, though now it had something of an hysterical edge to it.

"Oh dear," Liseth said after she managed to calm herself, wiping the tears from the edges of her eyes. "I've been such a fool, haven't I?"

Sasuelana looked more alarmed than timid. "What are you talking about?"

"You've always manipulated me, haven't you?" Liseth said, giving the other a warm smile to take the sting out of her words. "I know that your timid act was just that, an act. But you've used it like a hunter with a net, to herd me the right direction."

Liseth could see it now, how Sasuelana had influenced her decisions. Through timid questions and misdirection, Sasuelana had always led Liseth to where she needed to be.

"I don't know what you mean," Sasuelana said, looking confused.

Liseth took a deep breath. Was Sasuelana unaware of how she'd prodded Liseth into action with her timid nature? Or was she a master manipulator? Would Liseth ever know?

"I know you won't come back to the temple," Liseth said. "Won't take up your old position."

"That's true my lady," Sasuelana said, nodding. "I'm having far too much fun with my grandkids." She gave a proud smile.

"However, could I ask, as an old friend, for you to come and visit with me once a week? Just for an afternoon, so we could talk?" Liseth said.

Sasuelana gave her a brilliant smile. "That would be lovely!" she said. "I would like that. But do you think we should meet here?"

Liseth recognized the mask that Sasuelana slipped on. Why had she never seen it before?

"I wouldn't want to hurt Ajooless, for her to think that her position wasn't assured," Sasuelana said, her voice quiet and almost quivering.

"You're right," Liseth said, nodding. "We should meet at the Wavy Crossroads," she added, naming one of her favorite teashops close to the temple. "Tomorrow afternoon? My treat," she emphasized.

"That would be lovely," Sasuelana said with an assured smile that transformed her face into something much more beautiful and powerful. "After the midday hour."

After Sasuelana had gone, Liseth sat in the empty sanctuary for a bit longer, thinking. She could never ask why Sasuelana had come to the temple that evening, what the other person had been praying for.

Had Sasuelana been praying for anything? Or had she just been lying in wait for Liseth to appear?

Liseth would never know. And while a part of her resented how much Sasuelana had probably manipulated her over the decades, another part of her was grateful for Sasuelana's guidance that had gotten her through so many tough times and decisions. That guidance would truly be a blessing now.

Or maybe it was divine providence at work. Liseth had come to the statue of the goddess to pray for help, after all…

Chapter Sixteen

WIND

KA LEM WORRIED as he raced along the curved paths of
Shan Yu, making his way as quickly as possible (while still in
Wind Person form) to the house of the elders. He wasn't sure
why they'd requested his presence so early in the morning the
day before all the warriors and hunters were leaving to go
investigate the wall.

Winter had taken firm hold of the land. Snow had fallen
the night before, but it had been trodden down along all the
paths, growing gray and sodden. A wan blue sky covered
with long strands of clouds made it seem even chillier to
Ka Lem.

The huts here in the capital sat much closer to one
another than the huts in Ka Lem's village, some so close that
two neighbors could reach out their windows and clasp
hands! He couldn't imagine always living so close to other
people. The houses followed the same form as those in his
village, rounded with wooden shingles and conical roofs
covered in moss. While the houses themselves were
frequently larger, the yards were much smaller. Then again,

the people in the capital had more markets to go to and so they grew less of their own vegetables in their gardens.

The celebration of light was only a few weeks away. Some of the houses he passed already had garlands of yew or holly draped over their doorways. Almost every merchant had candles for sale, as the Wind People would dance and pray through the entire night, feasting come sunrise.

Where would Ka Lem be when the festival started? He'd planned on being back in Killapany for the festival this year, after taking on the soul form of an elk.

Would he be at war this year instead? Fighting for his life instead of dancing? The thought chilled him. Though Ka Lem never talked about it, he still sometimes felt the female bear deep inside him stir. Mostly she kept him light on his feet, prodding him to dance, but sometimes she would give a warning growl as she just had.

Shivering, Ka Lem continued along his path to the house of the elders. The attendants ushered him inside immediately to the meeting room.

A young person stood in front of the seated elders, shivering. She wore a brown robe over her shoulders, though she hadn't belted it. She was about the same age as his sister. She had skin the color of wet oak, as much gray as brown, with a riot of curls and cool blue eyes.

Was she cold? No, not given the wide terror around the edges of her eyes, the way her mouth gaped.

"Ka Lem," Hi Lop said as soon as he entered. "Would you please do us a favor?"

"Of course," Ka Lem said, stepping beside the young person.

"Can you take the form of a wolf? One larger than usual?" Hi Lop said.

Ka Lem blinked, surprised. That had *not* been what he was expecting at all.

He quickly slipped off the heavy felted-wool jacket that his host had loaned him, as well as the soft green shirt and gray pants, kicking off two sets of socks and then his boots, as the only shoes he'd been able to borrow had been too large for him.

Once unhindered by clothing, Ka Lem reached for the form of the wolf.

Fear struck him as he found an achingly familiar cold where the form should be.

Sweat broke out across his bare back. He didn't want to reach into that cold emptiness again. But he made himself do it, made himself grab onto the form of a wolf.

The transformation was more difficult than it should have been. It felt as if his Wind Person form fought the change. He had to force the hair out from his smooth skin, punch the snout out of his flat face, even push his muscles around so that they fit inside a wolf's body.

As color fled from the world and scent filled in all the spaces, he knew that he'd succeeded in finding the wolf's true form.

Ka Lem took a few paces back and forth, settling into the warmth and fierceness of the wolf's heart.

Finally Hi Lop said, "You can change back, now."

Ka Lem nodded and flowed back into his Wind Person form. It was much easier than the initial transition to the wolf had been.

"Tell us how that felt," Hi Lop commanded.

Ka Lem did, telling them of his initial dread that the wolves had been taken, of the difficulty he'd had transforming.

"It is as we've feared," Hi Lop said when he finished. "We suspect the Bone People might be trying to take the form of the wolf." She paused, then answered his unasked question.

"It was the form Gan Ou was in when she first went through the wall."

That made a terrible sort of sense. Ka Lem felt torn between fear that the Bone People would succeed and anger that they were even trying.

"We need to instruct each village to get a volunteer to take the soul form of the wolf. Perhaps one of the reasons why the Bone People haven't been successful in stealing the form is because too many of the Wind People still cling to it," Hi Lop said.

"What can I do to help?" Ka Lem said.

"Instruct the warriors and the others leaving to confront the wall tomorrow that the form of the wolf may no longer be safe. They should consider some other form before they enter," Hi Lop replied. She paused. Some other thought made her eyes widen.

"Thank you, Yan May," Hi Lop said, dismissing the girl. "You did the right thing coming to tell us right away."

The young person gave a slow nod, then turned and walked out of the council room reluctantly, as if she wanted to stay and listen.

After she'd gone, Hi Lop turned to the other council members. "We need to show him. Possibly it's a form that the Bone People will never expect."

Ka Lem watched the other elders shift in their seats, uncomfortable. Show him what?

Again, it seemed to him that a wind flitted around the various elders, carrying snatches of conversation that he couldn't quite make out.

The elders came to a silent agreement, the decision resting heavily on their shoulders. One of the others called out to the attendant standing next to the door, "Go fetch Ao Shur."

Ka Lem blinked, surprised. It couldn't be the same Ao Shur he'd known in Killapany, was it?

But it was. He gave Ka Lem a wide grin. Though he was about ten years older than Ka Lem, he seemed much younger. His skin was a light brown color, with bright green eyes. He worked with wood in Killapany, traveling every spring up into the mountains to supervise which trees were taken, then spending the fall and winter making both practical things like wooden doors and shutters, as well as beautiful carvings.

Ka Lem didn't know all of Ao Shur's story, why he'd stayed in Killapany after his teacher training instead of returning home. It might have been the wood, though, as the forests high in the mountains of the Stone People held different types of trees than the woods of the Wind People.

He wore a robe that would be easy to slip out of, obviously ready to change into another form quickly.

Under one arm he carried a large book. From a quick glance, Ka Lem judged it to be a children's book, one used to teach the young ones the different animal forms.

"Show him. Teach him," Hi Lop commanded.

Ao Shur nodded, as if he'd been expecting this. He carefully opened the book, using gentle and reverent hands. Ka Lem immediately reached out and helped support the open book.

The smell of mold and ancient paper made him wrinkle his nose. The watercolor paintings in the book were done using an older style. Picture book figures were made with much more crispness now, the outlines thicker.

Ao Shur pointed to the form on the open page, naming it, "A horse."

Ka Lem blinked. He'd never seen that form before.

Before he could ask, Ao Shur continued. "It's been taken, like the elk," he said.

Ka Lem couldn't help the shiver that made his shoulders twitch. However, his fear was quickly replaced by anger.

How dare they?

"They didn't get all of them." Ao Shur pointed to a different breed, up in the corner. "It's called a pony."

Ka Lem studied the figure intently. The coat looked shaggy and brown. It also appeared to be stockier compared to the other horses, as well as much smaller and shorter, about the size of a small deer.

"Let me show you," Ao Shur said.

Ka Lem took the ancient text from Ao Shur, cradling it carefully, then stepped back to give him room.

Ao Shur slipped his robe off, placing it on top of the neat pile of Ka Lem's clothing, then changed into the form of a pony.

Ka Lem could tell that it took some effort on Ao Shur part. Was it because the form was so foreign? Or because so many of its relations had been taken?

After gently closing the book, Ka Lem reached out one hand to touch the strange creature now standing in front of him. The coat wasn't completely smooth, but possibly if it was brushed regularly it would be. It had a short, muscular neck with a rough mane running down it, wide eyes that appeared almost liquid brown, and a rounded body with strong legs, ending in hooves.

Ka Lem closed his eyes for a moment, searching. It didn't take him long to find the form. He'd have to practice it a few times, but he was certain that he could take this shape when needed.

When Ka Lem opened his eyes again, Ao Shur had already transformed back into his Wind Person shape.

"Thank you for sharing this with me," Ka Lem said gravely as he returned the book to Ao Shur. Then he turned to face the elders again.

"Go practice," Hi Lop told him. "Then teach the others. This may be the form you should take when you travel through the wall, something that whoever is on the other side may not be expecting."

"I will," Ka Lem said, his words sounding strangely fervent to his own ears. He held back the rest of his questions, such as, when had this form disappeared? Had the Stone People discovered the ancient book? They must have, otherwise why would Ao Shur have it?

But the most important question of all still seemed to echo through the room: what other forms had the Wind People lost over the centuries?

Ka Lem bowed low to the elders when he saw that he'd been dismissed.

So many questions. But finally, it was time for some action.

KA LEM WAS surprised when he saw Gan Ou standing with the group of warriors and hunters traveling to the wall. Why was she there? Did she honestly think they wouldn't be able to find it on their own?

Then he saw the determined look on her face, and flushed with shame.

No, it was nothing like that.

She was just as determined as the rest of them to figure out this mystery, to get back at whoever was on the other side of the wall and burning everything.

The day was overcast, and the iron smell in the air promised more snow later that afternoon. Hopefully they'd be flying out of the storm and not into it. The group of twenty-seven (three times three times three—one of the luckiest numbers known) gathered outside the hut of the elders. They would be picking up more people at the villages as they passed over, swelling their group to eighty-one by the time they reached the wall.

While none of the animals that the Wind People knew could count as the Wind People did, many had some rudimentary understanding of numbers. Three was always the indicator of more intelligent animals. Two was easy to understand. Three took more effort. In addition, there were three gods, three People.

Ka Lem had listened to the arguments one of the priests had made the night before, after drinking too much beer, that that their count was off. There were actually four People, and possibly four gods.

Just the thought had given rise to more nightmares for Ka Lem.

Though Ka Lem wasn't a hunter, he was considered one of the council of leaders, as he'd been the one to discover the elk were missing, and then had proven himself a serious young person with good ideas. Not all who'd volunteered to go were selected by the elders. Only one of the others from Ka Lem's home village had made the final cut.

They weren't an army. They were scouts, meant to breach the wall in several different locations to gain information, then bring it back. The elders had already set up a messenger system so that no one had to fly all the way back to the capital on their own.

Ka Lem stamped his feet with the rest of the group as the priests and priestesses gave their blessing to the group, wishing them light from Sune Li, strength from Kiproary, and the great wisdom of all the ages of Ishkra.

As one, all twenty-seven shrugged off their coats and robes, standing naked in the chilly square. They left their robes where they were, puddled on the ground. Wings started sprouting. Loud squawks rang through the air. In a short while, a large flock of black-headed geese stood among the dropped clothing. They had black heads and necks, with a white streak under their chins and brown bodies.

Normally, a black-headed goose stood about three feet tall. These were taller than usual, with many of them having a seven-foot wingspan.

They all took to the air, quickly assuming a familiar V-shape. The strongest would lead for a while, then fall back and others would take their turn.

Ka Lem fell into an open space, feeling his wings stretched out wide. Hopefully, they'd get a good tail wind and be able to make good time. He opened his mouth now and again to catch any bugs that might happen to be this high, though he knew, given the weather, there wouldn't be many.

It would take the group only a few days to reach the wall, even though they'd have to rest every night. From there, they'd split up into smaller groups, each with their own section to breach. Each group would select the forms they'd take, several of them would appear as poines. They'd all meet again a few miles away, in a spot yet to be determined, then fly back to the capital.

Hopefully, not all of them would be shot at immediately, and they'd actually see what was on the far side of that wall.

Chapter Seventeen

STONE

NOALANON SNUGGLED CLOSER TO JOLAPEN. They were wrapped around each other, naked, skin on skin, recovering from their earlier play. The phosphorous spots on the ceiling had already faded, leaving their bedroom in shadows, hiding the two wooden dressers full of clothes (because Jolapen insisted on having zir own), the single painting of the five of them hanging in a place of honor over the cozy wooden bed, even the colorful quilt draped over the pair of them.

I will miss this.

The words echoed strangely and seemed to come from outside of Noalanon, though ze knew neither of them had spoken out loud.

Had it been zir thought? Or had it come from Jolapen? And what did ze mean by it?

Jolapen lifted Noalanon's face up with a gentle finger and kissed zir lips tenderly. "Do you know when you'll leave?"

Noalanon held zirself very still for a long moment before ze chuckled. Ze shook zir head and cuddled closer to zir partner. "I hadn't actually decided to go. Not until just now."

It was Jolapen's turn to chuckle. "I knew you'd be leaving the moment you first talked about it. It isn't in your nature to stay."

"What do you mean?" Noalanon asked. They had discussed it earlier, about Noalanon volunteering to travel with the others to the wall, to show their support of the Wind People. But really, it had just been a possibility. Noalanon hadn't made the decision. Had ze?

Jolapen kissed zir again. "You remember when we first met?"

Noalanon nodded slowly. "It was at a midsummer party." They'd both just finished their schooling. Noalanon had returned from zir studies in the Sea People's land, and was so happy to be home at last. At that point, ze had sworn to never leave again.

"Some idiot made a derogatory comment about how irresponsible the Wind People were. You wouldn't let that slide," Jolapen said. "You were never going to convince that idiot that they were wrong. But you were determined to try." Ze kissed Noalanon's temple. "I may have fallen in love with you at that moment."

Noalanon snorted. "What, because I was stubborn about being right?"

"No, because you wouldn't let an injustice stand," Jolapen correctly gently. "Which is why I knew what your decision would be, even before you did."

Noalanon snuggled closer to zir partner. "I love you," ze said softly.

Jolapen pulled zir even closer. "You are my light. My hearthstones. And my home," ze said softly. "You are my everything. But I also know that you need to do this. You need to go see this injustice set right. Just promise me you'll come back."

"I will," Noalanon said, kissing zir partner fervently. "I, too, will miss this."

It wasn't until long afterwards, when they were both satisfied again and Noalanon was able to drift in zir own thoughts, wondering at zir luck at finding such a good partner, at how close they'd become, able to share unspoken thoughts occasionally, and ignoring the tiny spike of fear at whether or not they'd lose that ability while ze was gone, never to regain it.

***

THOUGH IT DISAPPOINTED Noalanon that so few of the Stone People had volunteered to go help the Wind People, it didn't surprise zir. The Stone People tended not to travel. There were very few of their kind who permanently lived in lands outside of their own territory, especially compared to the Wind and Sea People.

The travelers had gathered in the main city square that last morning, a few blocks away from the council chambers. Clear sky shone overhead, intensely blue and free of clouds. Despite the bright sunlight, snow still packed the street and stood piled up in the shadows, casting the city in grays, blacks, and white.

Five carts would carry the Stone People over the land. The carts were long and narrow, with two axles. A pair of raised boxed were at the front where the people would sit. They traveled four to a cart, each pulled by a team of smaller oxen that were favored by merchants both for their speed as well as their endurance. Minerals, blankets, sleeping pads, and trunks for clothes were piled at the back of each long wooden cart, covered with oiled tarps.

While it was possible for a Stone Person to run, they

tended not to move quickly. Plus, they had to carry their own food with them. Though a Stone Person didn't have to eat much, they still needed at least a couple of spoonfuls of their own special minerals every day or else they'd slowly starve.

Noalanon already sat in zir spot on the front bench of a cart. They weren't covered, as the Stone People didn't care if it rained, snowed, or was boiling hot—they didn't need protection from the elements unlike the other people. At least three fourths of the other travelers had taken their places as well and were just waiting to leave.

Jolapen and the children had said their tearful goodbyes in the privacy of their own home. It appeared that most of the other travelers had done the same and sat without their families in the square.

Three priests came out to bless each cart, sprinkling finely ground stone from the holy mountain on the wheels. The council members followed after the priests, thanking the travelers for their sacrifice.

Finally, they were ready to go. Noalanon was surprised to find the tears in zir eyes as the cart lurched and started rolling away. Then again, perhaps they weren't zirs, but belonged to Jolapen and the rest of the family. Ze had gotten so close to zir partner these last few days.

Ze took a deep breath of the clean air, glancing over zir shoulder at the holy mountain. In a few days, ze wouldn't be able to see it anymore.

Then Noalanon faced forward, determined. As Jolapen said, there was an injustice to right, a thing that needed doing.

Though Noalanon already missed zir home, ze knew that ze wouldn't return until ze'd set things right.

NOALANON WASN'T positive when the carts crossed over the border of the Stone People and into the lands of the Wind People. They were still in the foothills of the mountains, zigzagging down, and the land hadn't grown completely flat.

However, when they called a halt for the day, and ze stepped down out of the cart and touched the ground for the first time that afternoon, ze knew that they had crossed the border.

The carts had drawn up into a clearing just past a small market town. They hadn't bothered stopping at the inn— there were too many of them, and they had brought their own bedding, plus awnings for keeping rain or snow from falling on them while they slept.

Noalanon stood at the side of the cart and shifted from one foot to the other, trying to determine what exactly was different.

The feel of the land had changed. Though Killapany's streets were all paved with stone, the pathways covered in gravel, the bare dirt here in the Wind People's territory felt harder and colder. It was as if it lay unyielding underneath zir feet instead of supporting them.

Was this what the Wind People felt when they were in the Stone People's territory? That the very ground itself no longer aided them? Ze had heard that complaint more than once, and had just assumed it was because the Wind People had very few paved paths, preferring pounded dirt instead.

Noalanon caught the eye of Daleki, who rode on a different cart. They had grown to become good friends over the last few days. Their skin color was almost the same, a pale gray, and they both tended to wear their long black hair in a loose pony tail, but Noalanon's eyes were the blue of summer skies and Daleki's eyes were an unusual color, golden, like amber.

Daleki was also a teacher, as were most of the other travelers. In addition, there were five merchants, four artists, a single miner, and a single builder.

The merchants were the ones who'd volunteered to drive the carts, though Noalanon and the others were learning how to take care of the animals. They'd split the tasks up equitably, each doing their assigned chores to get the evening's camp established.

Daleki nodded at Noalanon. They'd talk later, after they'd gotten the camp set up. They'd been lucky so far, missing the snow. Given the gray swollen clouds overhead and the smell of the air, Noalanon suspected they wouldn't remain that lucky for long. All around them, the tall pines sang in the wind and the dried grass waved and bowed.

Noalanon helped set up the awnings, then piled the bedding and blankets under the primary covering so that people could select their own and choose their place to lie down. Others set up bowls and uncovered the containers of minerals at the back of one of the carts. People would scoop up what they needed that day, as the ratio of what they required changed frequently depending on the individual.

Water had been their most pressing concern, as the stream the road ran along had grown dry in some places. When they'd found pure water again, they'd stopped and filled up every container they had so that they wouldn't run out.

Finally, the evening chores done, after Noalanon filled a small bowl with zir evening minerals, ze went to find Daleki. Noalanon couldn't help but grin when ze found zir friend sitting on zir bedding to one side, Noalanon's spread out beside it.

"Thank you," Noalanon said as ze sat down. Though ze had been sitting on the cart for most of the day, it still felt good to finally sit on the ground and rest.

Although—it wasn't as restful as it had been before.

Before Noalanon could say anything, Daleki asked, "You feel it too, don't you?"

Noalanon nodded.

"Like you, I've traveled through these lands before. I didn't notice any difference, except that I tired more easily," Daleki said. "But now…"

"The Wind People frequently complain that the land of the Stone People isn't as friendly," Noalanon said. "I wonder if this is what they meant. That the very ground itself isn't as supportive."

"It could be," Daleki said. "The merchants don't seem to care. However Hirshamin, the builder, appears to be truly affected."

Noalanon looked at the others, trying to spot the builder. Ze had a broad build, broader than most. Ze also wore zir hair pulled back into intricate braids along the side of zir head.

Hirshamin appeared to have some difficulty standing up straight. Ze seemed to be leaning, first to one side, then the other.

Noalanon and Daleki weren't the only ones to notice, however, and more than one concerned traveler had come over to speak to Hirshamin, urging zir to sit down.

"I've never seen anyone react that way," Noalanon said, thinking of zir first trip to the land of the Wind People.

"I haven't either," Daleki said. "I have heard of it before, though. A land-sickness. They can't leave the mountains, or their home village. It pains them to stay on land that is unknown to them."

"Huh. I have heard of that as well," Noalanon said after a moment. "I didn't think it was real," ze confessed.

"I knew of someone who swore that zir sibling had it," Daleki said. Ze shrugged. "Supposedly, that was why zir sibling hadn't been able to become a teacher, even though that was the path zir heart had been set on."

"Interesting," Noalanon said. "Do you think that teachers somehow self-select, for the most part? That only those who can travel become interested in the profession?"

"I don't know," Daleki said. "We weren't the only teachers who noticed the land had changed."

"But why didn't I notice it before, though? The first time I traveled?"

Daleki shook zir head. "I've been puzzling on that and haven't figured it out yet."

"Maybe it's just acclimation," Noalanon said. "We've already been exposed to the difference between the two lands, and so were already more sensitive."

"Then wouldn't the others have felt the same way?" Daleki asked. "It isn't age, as we aren't the oldest or the youngest among the teachers, but about in the middle."

Noalanon thought for a while, carefully eating zir minerals from zir bowl. "Do any of the others have families? Children?"

Daleki looked at the others, making the same list in zir head that Noalanon had. "Maybe?" ze said after a moment. "I'm not sure. But we're both Manas, right?"

Noalanon couldn't hide zir gasp. "Do you think that's the difference?"

Daleki shrugged. "It could be. We'll have to ask around, later."

Noalanon gave a sigh, but nodded. It wasn't a question that would be easy to pose, as it was rude to inquire whether a person was a Mana or a Baba to their children. However, ze was certain that ze could get to the bottom of this mystery.

IT TOOK a couple of days of careful inquiry for Noalanon and Daleki to determine that their theory was right. The people who were most affected by being in the Wind People's territory were the Manas in the group. None of the Babas felt any change at all. There were a few people who had no partner or family either, so were neither a Mana or a Baba. They also didn't feel the difference in the earth.

It turned out Hirshamin, in addition to being a builder and more closely associated with the earth than the others, had also given birth to two sets of twins, which was almost unheard of. Ze had made jokes about getting away from all the teenagers in zir house.

Noalanon and Daleki spent time discussing the issue, though the others tended not to join in. The subject made everyone uncomfortable. The Stone People were genderless, and almost everyone could grow a child. The idea that something fundamentally changed in them after the birth was disturbing. There shouldn't be anything different about them. That came too close to there being gender distinction among the Stone People. Yet, there was.

Perhaps it was something in the special minerals they had to consume in order to start a child, something that tied them closer to the land. That was the only thing that made sense to either Noalanon or Daleki.

The weather had grown slightly warmer as they moved west and south, though it had also grown steadily wetter. Noalanon felt as though ze was always warming zir core. The oxen didn't like the slippery ice and snow on the roads either. More than once a cart would get stuck in the mud and everyone would have to get out to help push it along.

Even being under the trees didn't seem to make much difference. Wind would knock heavy clumps of snow onto them. Noalanon tried to keep zir spirits up. Ze thought about Ka Lem, and how brave he'd been flying between the various capitals, carrying the news. He hadn't complained about being hungry and tired, driving himself to the end of his endurance.

It only helped so much, however.

Noalanon tried walking beside the cart for a while, but it took too much effort for ze to keep up with the quick-stepping oxen. Ze wasn't the only one who'd tried. Hirshamin could trot faster than the others, despite zir stout build and shorter legs.

Finally, they reached Shan Yu. Noalanon was surprised at how different it looked from zir memories. The houses seemed so small and quaint, covered in wood and snow. They also looked as if the first strong winds of spring would blow them over. Too many trees lined the road, making the city seem gloomy. No elegant stone carvings or statues brightened the way.

The merchants drew the cars up to the main square of the city, though to Noalanon, it just looked like a big open space without decorations or fountains to lighten the heart.

Someone had informed the elders that the travelers were coming, and so all nine of them had already gathered in the square to greet them.

"Welcome! Welcome!" came the glad cries.

Noalanon hadn't met Hi Lop before—a short, squat person with skin the color of baked brick, her black curly hair shot through with gray. She wore a heavy brown robe over her clothes, along with a long white scarf knitted in an intricate pattern.

"What brings so many of the Stone People to our lands this gray afternoon?" Hi Lop asked, stepping forward.

Though the travelers hadn't selected a single representative, Noalanon found zirself the only one who to speak. "We heard the news of the wall and fires encroaching on your lands," ze said plainly. "Though only a few of us made the initial journey, we wanted you to know that the Stone People support you. We travelers are here to offer what aid we can."

A sound of awe traveled through the crowd. Noalanon thought it was misplaced. If there were a hundred or more Stone People who'd braved the foreign lands, wet roads, and winter conditions, that would be one thing. Merely twenty barely warranted any respect at all.

"Our warriors have already left, just this morning," Hi Lop informed them. "Would you follow after them?"

Noalanon quickly said, "Yes," before any of the other of the Stone People could reply.

Hi Lop gave zir a sharp nod. "So it will be," she announced.

The oxen were quickly removed from the carts, while hot water and spiced tea were brought for the Stone People to consume.

Noalanon found zirself holding zir cup up to deeply inhale the scent. Ze had had this drink during zir teaching year, but not since. It almost brought the sense of home to zir. Others among the travelers did the same, particularly the teachers.

Hi Lop stood beside Noalanon and looked at the travelers. "I was not a teacher," she said softly. "So I do not know your ways. I know that you are much stronger than any of the other People. However. Forgive my question, but do you have any hunters in your group?"

Noalanon gave her a quick grin. "Hunters, no." The leather used for their goods came from animals that had been raised for the purpose, not hunted down. "Were you aware that regular arrows cannot pierce our skin?"

It was almost comical how wide the Wind Person's eyes grew. "No! I didn't. How?"

Noalanon held out zir arm and willed the skin there to grow harder. "Here. Touch here first, then here," ze said, indicating first the hardened part of zir forearm, then above the elbow where the skin remained soft. Noalanon and the other travelers had all been practicing on their journey to Shan Yu, until the transformation was quick and easy.

"It's like stone," Hi Lop said in wonder.

Noalanon grimaced. The hardened skin wasn't, not really. Stone was much harder. It was still possibly to damage the skin, particularly with obsidian knives. Plus, unlike stone, such skin wouldn't shatter or break.

"Thank you for showing me that," Hi Lop said. "And thank you for coming, without us asking," she added.

Noalanon nodded. Ze understood that the Wind People never would have asked for help, primarily because it never would have occurred to them. If they'd started fighting a war and were losing, they might ask for help, but then again, their pride might prevent them.

It didn't take long for the carts to be re-harnessed with new oxen. However, these weren't animals, but Wind People who'd taken on the form of oxen, who would be able to travel much more swiftly. The Wind People's food, clothing, and bedding were added to the back of the carts. Suddenly, it was time for the travelers to be on their way.

Priests and priestesses came out to bless the carts, the travelers, the Wind People working with them.

Hi Lop then added, "You have the blessings of the Wind and Stone People. May your journey be speedy and uneventful. May you quickly return home with many marvelous stories."

The new oxen took off at a sharp pace. Noalanon marveled at how much faster they now traveled.

They soon passed out of the village and were under the

trees again. Noalanon raised zir head, trying to see if ze could smell smoke.

It would come all too soon, ze suspected, dread overtaking zir as they zipped along, every step taking zir farther from zir home than ze had ever been before.

Chapter Eighteen

SEA

LISETH SAT at a table in the Wavy Crossroads, calmly sipping her tea and waiting for Sasuelana. The teashop was one of her favorites. It held a dozen round tables with three to four chairs at each. The floor was plain red tiles, but the walls were covered in beautiful tapestries and quilts with geometric patterns. A single counter stood way at the back of the room, looking more like a carved podium. The kitchen, where the tea was made, lay behind the counter.

This shop brewed a spicy warm tea with ginger and peppers during the winter, while summer teas were frequently chilled and flavored with rosehips, lavender, or lemon balm. They had several different seaweed and green-tea bases, going from bitter and smoked to light and sweet.

It didn't irk Liseth to be kept waiting, though it was quickly approaching the second hour after the midday meal. She used the opportunity to study the others who sat around the cozy glass tabletops held up with elegantly curved iron legs, making a game of guessing occupations or who they waited for.

There were at least a couple of dozen other people in the

shop, leaving only a few tables empty. The young female in the corner was obviously waiting for her sweetheart, though she tried to hide just how nervous she was. Two older females sitting at the table beside her gossiped non-stop, probably about their shared acquaintances. A very young male sat at one of the larger tables at the back, surrounded by half a dozen children and looking harried as he tried to control them, waiting for his acquaintance as well.

There were others—the group who'd taken over three tables and were studying, as well as the older male who wasn't waiting for anyone, merely taking in the afternoon, quietly reading his book as he sipped his tea.

No one bothered Liseth. She was certain that they all knew who she was. As the high priestess of the main temple in the city, she couldn't go anywhere and be anonymous. Not that she needed to hide her actions. After all, she was waiting for her dear old acquaintance. Nothing suspicious in that.

Yet…the edges of this meeting held the taste of something illicit. Was it because Liseth was expecting Sasuelana to try to manipulate her unknowingly? Or was it because Liseth desperately needed such guidance?

Liseth still hadn't made the decision about which route to use to send any volunteers. The choices were just too even, with equal pros and cons.

Finally, Sasuelana hurried into the shop. She waved at Liseth and went directly to the counter to fetch her own tea before scurrying over to where Liseth sat. She wore an older blue dress that day that showed where rips had obviously been repaired. It still looked lovely against bluish skin.

It reminded Liseth once again that Sasuelana was no longer working at the temple. She would never have worn something so old or worn there.

Of course, that meant that Sasuelana had done it deliberately, to remind both of them of her current place.

"I'm so sorry for being late!" Sasuelana blurted out before she even sat down. "So, so very sorry! But the littlest wouldn't settle down for his nap."

"You could have brought him with."

Sasuelana snorted. "No, I couldn't have. You've never raised any children. We wouldn't have been able to talk with him here."

Liseth had to concede that Sasuelana might have a point. Though Liseth had interactions with children, she'd never been around them that often. Her own siblings were much younger than she was and they'd never spent that much time together, even after they'd started their own families.

"Who did you leave the children with?" Liseth asked, suddenly concerned.

"The next door neighbor offered to keep an eye on them while I came here," Sasuelana said with a smile. "Don't worry," she added, patting Liseth's hand. "I do the same thing for her often."

Liseth turned her hand over to grip Sasuelana's. Though the Sea People held hands all the time with each other, particularly in their water form, Liseth had never encouraged that type of familiarity with anyone except Bayaseth.

Sasuelana gave Liseth a huge grin. "Thank you," she said, squeezing her hand tightly.

Liseth understood what Sasuelana meant, that she was thanking Liseth for allowing Sasuelana to change roles from being merely an acolyte to becoming a trusted friend.

"How are you today?" Sasuelana said after taking another sip of her tea.

Liseth blinked, surprised. What was Sasuelana doing? Why wasn't she asking about Liseth's problems?

"I'm fine," Liseth said. She took a deep breath. "A little tired." She was actually exhausted, weary to the bone. She was afraid that if she changed into her sea form, the edges of her scales might appear cracked.

Sasuelana squeezed Liseth's hand and looked expectantly at her.

"How are you?" Liseth said after a moment.

Sasuelana gave her a wide smile. "I'm good. But these little ones will be the death of me yet." She launched into a story about chasing the two older girls down that morning, getting them settled and eating breakfast, only to then have to wrangle the other three.

It took Liseth a while to figure out what Sasuelana was doing. If their friendship was to be real and not merely a convenience, then they had to do things like ask about each other's day and then listen, not merely wait for their opportunity to speak.

Liseth found herself smiling at her new friend as she wound down.

"Gracious, you're not here to listen to me blather about my grandchildren," Sasuelana said after a bit.

"I'm here to listen to whatever you have to say," Liseth said.

"Bless you," Sasuelana said, giving Liseth's hand a quick squeeze. "I might have needed this too, you know. A friend to talk with, who isn't either my children or grandchildren."

"Good," Liseth said. It did make her feel better to know that Sasuelana would be getting something out of their meeting together as well.

"So tell me what is going on outside of the city," Sasuelana said.

Liseth did, telling her about the wall that had been discovered, how the Wind People would be going to examine it. How the Stone People were probably going to send people as well, and that the Sea People needed to do the same.

"A lot has happened, then," Sasuelana said, nodding. "I'm assuming that you'll be asking for volunteers?"

"Aye," Liseth said. "But then comes my predicament. Which way do I send them? Along the southern route, which may be faster but more dangerous? Or along the more traveled roads to the north, that is likely to be much slower?"

Sasuelana looked puzzled. "Why not both?" she asked.

"Why not…Of course," Liseth said. She'd been too fixed on a single path, a single way. All of the Sea People knew that there were generally more than one answer to a question, more than one solution to a problem.

Had Bayaseth been correct in her judgement of Liseth? That she'd grown too stuck in her ways, instead of flowing between options as the Sea People generally did?

"Thank you, my friend," Liseth said. She could see the solution now. She would have to ask for volunteers for both routes. The southern route wouldn't attract as many of the Sea People, but there would still be some.

Could she set it up as a challenge? Get the two groups to compete? To see who could get to the lands of the Wind People the quickest? Possibly.

"Yes," Sasuelana said, watching Liseth carefully. "Sometimes two heads are better than one."

They walked out of the shop together after they finished their tea, holding hands, ready to face their own personal challenges. They'd already set a date for their next meeting in a week's time.

Liseth found herself smiling as she walked back to the temple and her office. Though a part of her was irked that Sasuelana had always been so timid around her while she'd been an acolyte, a part of Liseth was overjoyed to have discovered that she finally had a friend.

AS LISETH SUSPECTED, no one who spent the majority of their time in their sea form volunteered to travel overland to the Wind People's territory. What did surprise her was how many of them volunteered goods for those going, such as solid waterproof backpacks that the Sea People used underwater, as well as harpoons, nets, and javelins generally used for hunting fish.

In addition, more people volunteered to go along the southern route than she'd anticipated, and so now she was having to change her lists and her supplies.

She sat behind her desk going through the scrolls, crossing out items using a thick graphite stick encased in wood. Her comfortable, throne-like chair wasn't as comfortable as it once had been, given the number of hours she'd been sitting on it the last few days. The tea on her desk had long grown cold. The midday meal bells had rung but Liseth hadn't bothered to go eat anything.

She remembered Ka Lem, and how he'd been driven to reach them, then to return to the Stone People carrying the news. He'd joked with her once about how he'd sleep when he was dead.

The words had seemed oddly prophetic. Though Liseth didn't plan on working herself to death, she could possibly see it from where she was sitting.

"Excuse me? My lady?" came a voice from the doorway.

Liseth blinked, looking up from her desk and her plans. The light had grown dimmer in the office. How late was it? She'd lost track of the bells.

Ajooless stood in the doorway, her dark blue skin casting her in further shadows. "May I come in?"

"Certainly!" Liseth said, beckoning her main acolyte and eventual replacement in.

Ajooless carried a tray that held a fresh pot of tea and two cups. Without asking, she picked up Liseth's cold cup and replaced it with the fresh cup. Then she sat herself down in front of Liseth's desk and waited.

Liseth smiled and wrapped her cold fingers around the mug, breathing in the aroma of mint, winter berries, and the deep green scent of tea made from special seaweed that only grew in the colder waters north of them.

"Thank you," Liseth said after she'd taken a few restorative mouthfuls. While Sasuelana may have been a master manipulator, her timid mask would never have allowed her to be so bold as to assume that Liseth needed tea, then to just make it and serve it.

"What can I do for you?" Liseth asked after rolling her shoulders a few times, getting herself to relax. "Do you have news?"

Ajooless sighed. "I do not," she said sadly. "I still haven't been able to share my trail with anyone. I know it's right, though. I know those are the home waters of the Bone People!"

Liseth gave the girl a tight smile. She knew that Ajooless had been trying so hard to communicate what she'd discovered. It turned out that she didn't share well.

Maybe that was a good quality for a high priestess, though. Liseth had also never learned the knack.

"I still…I still want to help," Ajooless said. She sat up straighter in her visitor's chair. "So I'm here to volunteer to be one of the travelers, to go to the land of the Wind People."

Liseth gave an involuntary click of surprise before she clamped her lips tightly together. While there had been more volunteers than she'd expected, there hadn't been so many that she'd turn anyone down.

"Are you certain?" Liseth asked eventually after taking a long gulp of her tea.

"I am," Ajooless said. "Maybe once I get closer to where

the Bone People are, I'll be able to point the way for someone else to find their headwaters."

"That actually makes sense," Liseth said grudgingly. She sighed. "The problem is, I don't want to lose you." Though no one talked about it, such a journey across land was going to be grueling. Liseth wouldn't be surprised to lose at least a quarter of those who journeyed to disease or fatigue.

"You won't," Ajooless said. "Plus, if I am to be head priestess someday, I need to have a better understanding of the Stone and Wind People. Traveling to their lands would further my education."

"True," Liseth had to admit. Ajooless would have better knowledge than even Liseth if she went on this journey. Plus, Ajooless would have to learn how to negotiate and compromise with those in the group she was traveling with. Ajooless was still learning diplomacy and politics, seeing the need for it much more as she got older.

"Are you certain?" Liseth asked again. She didn't want to lose her replacement. She'd actually have to start training a new one once Ajooless left, just in case she didn't come back.

"I am," Ajooless said. She gave Liseth a wide smile. "I've even already talked my parents into agreeing."

"Really?" Liseth said, impressed. Ajooless's parents were very conservative and feared anything new. It had taken Liseth over a week of visits, carrying many gifts, for them to agree to Ajooless coming to study under Liseth at the main temple. Liseth would have thought that becoming the main acolyte at the temple and possibly the head priestess would have been enough of a draw, but Ajooless's parents had wanted her to stay at home and take care of them as they aged.

That was frequently the pattern among the Sea People. The older children would get married and provide many grandchildren, while the youngest would stay at home and look after the parents.

"They really did agree," Ajooless said. "I also got my two older sisters to agree to look in on them twice a week. So they won't be alone."

"Very good," Liseth said. Ajooless had really come a long way from the sullen teenager she'd first met.

"So can I go?" Ajooless asked.

Liseth smiled. Her impatience made her sound more like her now sixteen years of age.

"Which route would you take?" Liseth asked, not giving her blessing just yet.

"The southern route," Ajooless said firmly.

"Why?"

"It makes the most sense. It's the most direct route," Ajooless said. "Plus, it will take us through villages that have rarely seen a Sea Person. It's an opportunity to meet real people, not those used to us."

Liseth blinked, surprised. She hadn't thought of that. "And to win them over?"

"Of course," Ajooless said seriously. "We are facing an unknown threat," she added. "We need as many allies as we can get. Yes, we are going to support the Wind People. But by doing that, we earn the support and trust of so many more."

"Very good, very wise," Liseth said. She had realized that the group of travelers would earn them much good will. She was pleased that Ajooless appeared to realize the same without Liseth having to point it out to her.

"So can I go?" Ajooless asked again.

"You may," Liseth said. "And with my blessing."

"All I really need is the blessing of Ishkra," Ajooless said slyly.

"I'm sure you'll all have Her blessing as well," Liseth said.

"Is there anything else you need?" Ajooless said, standing. She looked critically at her mentor. "Did you eat today?"

"I had breakfast," Liseth said defensively.

"I'll bring you some soup," Ajooless said. "And more tea."

"Thank you," Liseth replied, feeling sheepishly younger herself. Then again, Ajooless was used to dealing with her parents, taking care of people older than herself.

Yes, life would be more difficult without Ajooless. Liseth would also have to find and train yet another replacement. But Liseth knew in her heart of hearts that this was the right choice. It never would have occurred to her to send her apprentice away, for her to travel with the others.

She wondered what Sasuelana would say about this new development.

Chapter Nineteen

WIND

KA LEM STRETCHED his arms wide, then swung them back and forth after he'd returned to his Wind Person form. It had been yet another long hard day of flying. The smell of smoke dominated all his other senses. The smell irritated Ka Lem, making him shake his head in whatever form he took. More than one Wind Person found themselves sneezing constantly, eyes watering and chest congested.

However, no one would turn back. Whatever was causing these fires wasn't natural. Given the amount of snow on the ground and being blown around by the winds, the dried grasses were too wet. They shouldn't be burning.

That night, the group of Wind People gathered in a huge clearing that was roughly triangular in shape. The two short sides were lined by tall pines, while a frozen creek marked off the third. All of the various groups of traveling Wind People were gathering together that night. The scouts and messengers they'd met with along the way informed them that the wall was close, only a day or so away.

Ka Lem was looking forward to the large gathering. While there was planning and organizing to be done, as well as forming their final groups and figuring out where each would be breaching the wall, there would also be dancing and singing.

After stomping his feet a few times, shrugging his shoulders and getting used to his person form again, Ka Lem walked over to where a huge mound of blankets, robes, and foot coverings awaited them at the edge of the clearing—a stash set up for them by the local villages so they could take on their own shapes for the evening. While Ka Lem's group had stayed with villages for most of the nights they'd been traveling, they hadn't the previous night, and so had stayed in animal form, changing into a large pack of wolves who'd slept curled up together, keeping each other warm. (The form had grown easier to take, which caused much speculation.)

The villagers had also supplied them with bows, arrows, and pikes. By the time Ka Lem approached the pile, most of the weapons had already been taken by those who hunted for a living. Ka Lem went into the forest with some of the others, gathering up dry firewood for the bonfires they'd have that night.

When he got back into the clearing, the rest of the Wind People had arrived. He greeted them all as friends, whether he knew their names or not.

It didn't take long for the deer, rabbits, and even fish to be put onto spits (more than one person had braved the frozen water and speared the immobile fish hibernating at the bottom of the river). Someone had also harvested winter apples in the forest, wrinkly and soft but mashed up with the bitter greens found at the water's edge made a good soup. The Wind People were good at foraging even in the winter, and so they also had nuts, frozen berries, and other foods to go with the meat.

Just before the feast began, a weird creaking noise echoed

through the clearing. Ka Lem stopped in the middle of his conversation to listen.

"What's that?" he heard people asking.

Ka Lem raced with the others toward the edge of the clearing. The hunters pushed their way to the front, arrows and pikes ready.

A cart, drawn by two small oxen, was approaching. No, not one cart. Four—Five carts!

Stone People sat on the long carts! Ka Lem recognized Noalanon immediately, sitting on the first one.

"Welcome! Welcome! Noalanon, welcome!" he called. Others following his example. "What are you doing here? Why have you come?"

"Patience," Noalanon said with a sly smile, teasing Ka Lem and the others.

All five carts came into the clearing and stopped. The Stone People immediately jumped down and started stripping the harnesses from their oxen. It only took a moment for Ka Lem and the others to understand what they were doing and more importantly, why. They rushed in to help.

As soon as the harnesses were removed, the oxen transformed into Wind People. Noalanon turned to Ka Lem and those designated as leaders of the group while the Wind People and the other Stone People started pulling their supplies from the carts.

"We were sent here from Shan Yu, by your elders, to accompany you through the wall," Noalanon finally told them. "Though this isn't a large group, the Stone People wanted to make sure that the Wind People knew that they were supported in their time of need."

Ka Lem knew that he wasn't the only Wind Person who suddenly had a lump in their throat. Though they'd been willing to face this unknown threat on their own, it was a relief to find out they had support.

"Thank you," said Ma Qi, the older female who'd informally become the primary leader. She was tall for a Wind Person, being five foot, eight inches tall. Her skin held more gray than brown, the light color of dried pine tree bark, and her eyes were pale gray as well. Her curly brown hair only held a few strands of silver, though Ka Lem knew she was over fifty. She had a calming presence that Ka Lem quite enjoyed. "Come, join us in our feasting!"

The Stone People quickly finished setting up their own camp, having their own meal before they joined the rest of the group.

Noalanon came to sit with the leaders of the Wind People, the group of nine who'd been informally designated "travel elders." They spent time assigning groups, dividing up the Wind and Stone People between them. Ka Lem marveled at how Noalanon's skin could grow hard.

They finally settled on their original number of nine groups, with three additional members added to each, two Stone People and one Wind Person, so each group was composed of twelve.

The remaining five Wind People would stay behind and guard their carts. The extra two Stone People would come with the main group that would penetrate the wall in roughly the same location as Gan Ou had gone through earlier.

After all the decisions had been made, Gan Ou came over to speak with Ka Lem and Noalanon. She still had a dour face and frowned constantly, though Ka Lem had caught her smiling more than once, a soft expression that always seemed to surprise the old person.

"Still getting into trouble, I see," Gan Ou said as she came up.

"Who, me?" Ka Lem asked, surprised. What had he done now?

"Eh, the both of ye," Gan Ou said with a sly smile.

"It's good to see you too," Noalanon said with a quick bow.

"I didn't think I'd miss it, you know," Gan Ou continued. "That stone capital of yours."

"It is beautiful," Noalanon said.

Ka Lem nodded. It had taken him a while, but he'd learned to see the beauty in the stone city. However, he didn't miss it one bit, not the way he'd missed his own small village.

"It's odd seeing you here, though," Gan Ou commented. "Out in the wild, away from the mountains."

Ka Lem had to agree. The Stone People looked out of place here in the lands of the Wind People. In their own country, they seemed natural, normal. Out here on the plain, even in the dim light of the huge bonfire, they looked more like moving piles of rock and less like people.

Did the Wind People have that same oddness to their appearance when they left their own lands?

Noalanon shuddered. "I miss the mountains more than you can know," ze said, zir voice suddenly hoarse. "And my family."

"Why did you leave them?" Ka Lem asked. He was so surprised that his former teacher had made such a long trip.

Noalanon gave him a soft smile. "It's what I do," ze said. "The wall, the smoke, the elk—it's wrong. And I do not suffer such things to exist." Zir voice grew fierce and determined.

Ka Lem wasn't sure he understood, but Gan Ou nodded. "Good on ye," she said. Then she sighed. "As strange as it is seeing you here, I'm glad you came. I'd like to send a message back to the capital with you, when you return. I'm…I'm staying here."

That made Ka Lem smile broadly. "Good," he said. He'd known that Gan Ou's banishment had been officially lifted, based on her service to the Wind People and the sacrifices she'd already made. Her skin hadn't fully healed yet, but that hadn't stopped her from making this trip, or even slowed her down.

Ka Lem had wanted Gan Ou to be one of the travel elders, but some of the Wind People still appeared to hold a grudge against her. Too many wouldn't have followed her, and so she was just an advisor.

"I shall miss your bright goods in the marketplace," Noalanon said sincerely.

"Oh, I still might send some things back, now and again," Gan Ou said. "This won't last forever."

Ka Lem didn't really consider Gan Ou's words until later that night, when he lay on his bedding and looked up at the sky, haze and clouds hiding the stars. He knew she was right, that their upcoming encounter wouldn't last forever. If they were lucky, the Wind People would poke through the wall, meet the other people there, and then each would turn away.

However, Ka Lem doubted that they were that lucky. There would be war. Hopefully Sune Li was on their side, Kiproary would support them, and Ishkra wouldn't turn her face away.

IT HAD TAKEN one more day of travel, as well as a few hours that morning, but now, Ka Lem and the others faced the massive wall. As Gan Ou had reported, it was too high to fly over. It had also moved at least two, possibly three days further west than when Gan Ou had first encountered it. No one knew why it had slowed down its westward march. Forests lay directly at their back. It was possible that either north or south, the wall had already entered the woods.

What lay on the other side? It was impossible to say. The smell of smoke lay heavy in the air, the haze turning the sun into a brilliant orange ball against the white sky. Ash swirled on the wind, easily mistaken for snow.

Ka Lem stood in the form of a pony between Gan Ou and Noalanon, with a brown coat as well as a shaggy brown mane and tail. The Wind People were mostly going to take the shape of ponies, though some had chosen other forms as well, such as deer, goats, and oxen. With the help of each other as well as the Stone People, robes and weapons had been strapped to their backs after they had changed.

The pony form had grown easier with practice, though it was still more difficult than most of the other forms. How had the Bone People missed the ponies? Were there variants of elks that the Wind People didn't know about who still existed elsewhere in the world?

No one knew where the ponies lived, though Ka Lem had heard the wild rumor that past the eastern shoreline of the continent, after crossing the huge ocean there, lay more lands. He'd never heard of such a thing before. It sounded like a comforting myth to tell children, though.

Gan Ou had retaken the form of a great wolf with a silvery coat and large blue eyes. He could still see where the wall had snatched out patches of fur, the skin covered with soft fuzz.

He only hoped that he would be as brave as she had been when it came time.

Ka Lem looked up and down the line of people standing with him. The Stone People would walk through the wall first, with the Wind People following them.

Noalanon gave him a nod and stepped forward, disappearing immediately into the thick mist.

Ka Lem and the others also stepped forward.

He was prepared for how cold the wall would feel. Gan Ou had warned them all of that.

What surprised him was how much wind swirled around him, circling his feet. Though it was the middle of the winter, the flavor of the winds reminded him of spring, how they gusted and blew.

While he didn't pause, he did see if he could find that spot Gan Ou had talked of, the place where there should have been more wind magic. He didn't find it in himself.

There appeared to be something else, though. Something to do with the trees and their leaves…

He couldn't concentrate on that. Not now. Instead, he focused outward, studying the surrounding area. The foggy wall wasn't pushing against him or denying him passage. Nor was it pushing him forward, either. It seemed more curious than anything else.

Suddenly, Gan Ou stood beside him. She appeared to be struggling, as if a solid headwind was blowing against her, trying to push her back.

Ka Lem walked directly in front of Gan Ou. Strong winds pushed against his chest and stirred his heavy coat, fluttering his mane, but then they died down. When he checked over his shoulder, Gan Ou gave him a wolfy grin. They started walking forward again, Ka Lem breaking the wind for her.

Others counted the steps it took to get through the wall. However, Ka Lem guessed that the wall had grown thicker as well, at least in this area, and that it took closer to two hundred paces to get through.

Exiting the wall of mist made him feel as though his ears had popped. He stretched his jaw and shook his head, trying to clear the sensation.

The smoke remained heavy on this side, as did the haze.

He paused and looked around, ready to race away if necessary, but no one shot at him.

With a quick shake, Ka Lem regained the form of a Wind Person. He stepped out of the belt that had been tied around his torso and picked up the robe and shoes. Others up and down the line did the same.

Noalanon stood some distance away, peering hard into the distance. "There's movement up ahead," ze announced.

Gan Ou just hrumphed. "So they're not watching the wall now," she muttered. "Of course they would only be doing that when I came through."

Ka Lem couldn't help but smile, a tense smile that also felt as though he were gritting his teeth.

The group quickly reformed. Three of the Wind People took flight, flying forward hard and fast. Another three, including Gan Ou, took the form of wolves and chased after them. The remaining six stayed together in a solid group, the four Stone People out front, their skin hardened.

They started moving forward. Ka Lem found himself wanting to gnash his teeth at their snail-like pace. He could hear Noalanon's voice telling him, "Patience" though, so he didn't say anything.

The wind shifted, carrying with it the sound of rattling chains and creaking wood. Ka Lem narrowed his eyes, trying to see where the sound was coming from.

Under the copse of trees in the distance, he saw figures moving. Though they were a good distance away, he knew they weren't Wind People. Their skin was too white, their hair, too blond. Goosepimples ran across his shoulders and down his back. The others beside him gasped when they came to the same realization.

He glanced at the other Wind People in the group. As one, they all started to run forward, leaving the Stone People behind.

They weren't spotted by the other people until they were halfway across the meadow. He heard the shouts, saw them pointing. A group of white and blond people ran out from under the trees.

The group bore javelins, knives, as well as bows and arrows.

Ka Lem wrenched his eyes away from the group racing toward them back to the ones under the trees.

The people who remained were traveling with large wooden carts, each at least ten feet long. The carts looked similar to the ones the Stone People used, though with only a single box at the front for people to sit on. White creatures with an unnatural gait pulled the carts forward.

It took Ka Lem a moment to realize that the corpses of the elk were drawing the four-wheeled carts along. They were cruelly chained to the vehicles with iron, each loop as long as Ka Lem's palm and two fingers thick. The racks of horns on the males were still on backwards, making their heads droop.

Red eyes blazed out of their naked skulls. Smoke rose up from the dead grass they walked on.

Were there no fires on this side of the wall? Or was it just the dead elk burning everything in their passing? How many of them were coming?

The Wind Person to Ka Lem's left suddenly stopped, turned, and started running back toward the wall.

It was time to leave. The hunters would engage the approaching warriors, while the rest *had* to take this news back to the elders.

Ka Lem had been one of those chosen to return instead of fight. He'd never been a hunter, so despite his protests, he'd been ordered to flee. Plus, he'd already proven himself a worthy messenger.

After one last long look, trying to quickly count the number of people he saw (over a dozen under the trees, and his nose told him there were many more) Ka Lem turned on his heel and started running back toward the wall.

Only to realize that a large group of the Bone People were already waiting for them, lying in ambush so they couldn't escape.

Ka Lem threw himself into the form of a great eagle, but it was too late. Weighted nets came crashing down on him, pinning him to the cold earth, unable to escape. A moment later, darkness overtook him.

KA LEM WOKE WITH A START. His head was ringing and his entire body ached, as if he'd been flying for three days straight. He was also in his Wind Person shape, though he didn't remember changing back. He lay naked on his back on the cold ground, shivering and trying to piece together what had happened.

Darkness surrounded him, the air full of shadows. It took him a few moments to realize it was just nighttime. The smell of smoke overwhelmed him. Clouds and haze filled the night sky. The only light came from the bonfire to his left. On his right, other shapes lay on the ground. Were those other Wind People? People from his group who had been captured?

How many had escaped? What had happened to the other groups? Had the Bone People captured the Stone People as well?

The clanking of chains rang out in the still night. Ka Lem pushed himself up on his elbow to see over the bodies.

Twenty feet away he saw the eerie glow of the elk, their bones giving off a soft blue light. Their eyes also still burned, bright red dots in the darkness. They were strangely still, standing all in a line, just shuffling their feet. The clanking chain had been looped over their necks and hung like steel necklaces from their bones.

"Get up," came a harsh voice. "All of ye."

Ka Lem saw a Bone Person standing just a few feet to his left. Ka Lem assumed it was a male given how broad his shoulders were, and that his torso went in at his waist, no hips to speak off. However, it wasn't easy to tell, as the person was fully clothed, wearing a long-sleeved shirt and trousers. A wide belt with bags hanging off it circled his waist.

"You're awake. Get up," the Bone Person ordered.

Only when Ka Lem drew his feet up did he realize that an iron shackle had been locked around his right ankle and a thick chain connected him to the others.

Didn't the Bone People realize that a Wind Person could transform into a creature that would cause the chains to suddenly fall from them?

Wait.

The word whirled around Ka Lem, carried on a gust of wind. He suddenly remembered the elders and how they seemed to talk without words. Someone in this group knew that trick.

He would have to learn how to do that as well. And soon.

The Wind People all rose to their feet unsteadily. It was too dark for Ka Lem to count how many stood with him, or to see if any of the Stone People were there as well.

"This way," the Bone Person said, turning and walking back toward the bonfire.

It took a few moments for the Wind People to coordinate with each other so that they could all walk together. None of them wore any clothes.

The iron felt oddly cold on Ka Lem's ankle. He resisted the urge to scratch at it. He had the image of himself as a strong wolf licking at it, gnawing it, worrying the skin near the iron clasped around his leg.

He shook his head and focused forward. He couldn't afford for his attention to wander.

Though this group was moving, traveling, it surprised him that they'd bring such a formal chair with them. No, not merely a chair, a throne, like what the kings and queens of the Sea People used to have. Even in the dim light of the bonfire Ka Lem could tell that it was intricately carved and painted, covered in vines and snakes, and possibly precious jewels.

The Bone Person himself—herself?—sat tall on the throne. He (probably) had blond curly hair that flowed like a mane around his head. His face had been covered with pale ashes, and he had black streaks down the center of his forehead and nose, plus harsh black lines drawn across his cheeks. The same black circled his eyes, making them seem deep and foreboding.

His clothing matched his face, primarily white with black patterns either sewn or painted on. The robe completely covered him from neck to wrist to ankle, with no belt.

He stood slowly, not because he was infirm, but because he wanted all their attention on him. Still, Ka Lem tried to see past the bonfire, past the throne. A large group of Bone People stood there, carrying spears and knives. It took Ka Lem a moment to realize that many of them had nets hanging from their waists, probably weighted ones like what had caught the Wind People.

Ma Qi stepped forward. "Who are you and why have you chained us like this?" she demanded, her voice strong. "Let us go."

Now Ka Lem could see that only half a dozen Wind People stood in the line. He thought he recognized many of the group that had been running with him. Where were the

Stone People? Had they gotten away? And the other six in his group, had they escaped as well?

"I am King Einar," he announced. His words had a strange lilt to them, almost a singing quality, though his voice was rough and hoarse. "You are chained because you are little better than animals. We have come to lead you out of your ignorance."

Ka Lem and the others looked at each other. What was this person talking about?

"We have the power over life as well as death," King Einar boasted. "Over all shapes and forms. Go ahead. Try to escape."

Ka Lem immediately reached for the first form he could think of, that of the large black-headed goose that they'd traveled in for so long. His ankle would shrink considerably, and the shackle should just fall away.

Except the form was gone.

Ka Lem raced through as many forms as he could. They all were out of reach. It felt as if he were cocooned in a thick wall of smoke, separated from all living creatures.

Wait, came the whispered word again.

At least that part of the Wind People's magic still appeared to be working.

"You see? We are mightier than you are. We have control over all the elements, while you barely work with a few," King Einar sneered.

"What would you teach us?" Ma Qi asked, sounding sincere, though her voice quavered slightly.

Not in fear. Ka Lem could tell that Ma Qi was furious, not afraid.

Ka Lem took a deep breath, despite the smell of ash and smoke. The Wind People were not about to be contained this easily. They would get out. Get away.

"Ah, my children," King Einar said, his voice gentling.

Ka Lem couldn't help the shivers that ran down his back at that tone. It sounded both patronizing as well as deeply threatening.

"You have so much to learn! Such as the strength of Valtyr, the god of my People," the king stated.

Ka Lem had never heard of such a god. The name sounded odd to his ears as well, as if King Einar swallowed the end of the word, and the "r" was merely a suggestion.

"How He has led us across the lands, to carry His word forward." The king chuckled at their obvious confusion. "Yes, Valtyr. The god your People so conveniently forgot." He turned stern again, like a scolding parent. "All of your myths talk of how your gods started in the darkness and pulled out of the abyss. Did it never occur to you that the darkness was ruled by a god as well?"

Ka Lem found himself frozen in fear. Were the Sea People right? Were the Bone People trying to usurp the other gods with their own?

"Before Sune Li came the darkness. Even you in your ignorance know that," King Einar said. He raised his hands over his head, fingertips touching. His eyes took on the red glow of the dead elk. "But you have forgotten the abyss, the actual birthplace of everything you know and love. You will remember, now."

Darkness flowed over Ka Lem. Filth and refuse coated his skin. The stench of rotting marsh waters and fetid fruit made him gag. When he made the mistake and tried to gasp, the blackness flew inside of him, filling his body with an inky darkness that he'd never be able to scrub clean.

Ka Lem choked, coughing and trying to vomit up the cold greasy night that now infected him. He heard the others beside him doing the same. He looked over at his companions as the darkness overwhelmed his vision.

Was this how King Einar saw them? Each of them had a

darkness that lived inside of them. All of them were fatally flawed, with death ticking away, each breath bringing them closer to that final embrace.

Only the bones shone through, white and pure.

His memories as a Wind Person were being eaten away by the darkness, consumed and tainted by filth. He couldn't remember the color of spring flowers, or the touch of soft wool on his bare skin. The smell of roasted venison was foreign to him, as was the sweetness of apples.

However, despite the cold blackness that surrounded them all, Ka Lem could also see a fire that burned deeply inside the heart of each of his companions. He assumed it was the lightness of Sune Li, that spark that gave them life.

All of King Einar's blackness and magic couldn't quench that fire.

Ka Lem took another deep breath, pushing past the burning in his throat, the vileness that now coated him. That spark was life. Lightness itself.

He couldn't find a creature to become, other than himself. So he reached for the bear who still lurked deep in his soul.

He didn't growl, or try to grow claws and maybe fight his way out.

Instead, Ka Lem remembered how light the bear was on her feet, how she danced in the snow under the two moons.

In defiance of the darkness surrounding him, Ka Lem started to dance, shuffling from one foot to another.

He didn't know how to convey that to the others, he didn't speak the Wind language, but they must have heard him anyway, because they all started to do the same, to step lightly either back and forth or side to side, hampered only by the chain connecting them and not by the inky darkness consuming them.

"What? What are you doing?" King Einar demanded.

"You—you shall not make light of my power! You shall not dance!" he bellowed.

Ka Lem didn't stop. King Einar might try to teach them all a darkness that Ka Lem didn't think he'd ever be able to forget, that would haunt him the rest of his days.

But this foreign king couldn't take away the dance that came from Sune Li.

Weighted nets landed on Ka Lem and the others, carrying them to the ground.

Ka Lem only had a few moments to wonder what the morning light would bring before the cold darkness overwhelmed him again.

Chapter Twenty

STONE

AS SOON AS Noalanon saw the strange white foreigners under the trees in the distance, ze turned to go back to the wall. The Wind People in their group had already left zir and the other Stone People behind, racing forward as impetuous as only the Wind People could be.

A group of Bone People crept up on them from behind, obviously an ambush.

Noalanon yelled, "It's a trap!" But ze doubted that any of the Wind People heard zir.

The individuals in the group of Bone People approaching them carried nets. They had hair that ranged from dark honey gold to stark white. Their skin was mostly white as well, with pink tinges to it. They were fully covered, from neck to wrist in mud-colored shirts, long black pants, and solid boots.

In addition to their nets, they also had knives stuck into their belts, as well as bows and arrows strung on their backs.

The three other Stone People who had turned around with Noalanon spread out in a line, forcing those coming for them to also divide up.

One group of Bone People raced past them, ignoring them and concentrating on the Wind People behind them instead.

Each of the four Bone People who remained deliberately aimed for a single Stone Person.

Noalanon had no idea how to fight. Ze had watched the Wind People grapple, but had never bothered learning.

Maybe it was a new skill that zir people needed to pick up.

The first of the warriors raced up toward zir and threw the net over zir head.

The net burned like ice, not like fire. Noalanon adjusted zir own temperature higher and kept walking, a deliberate slow pace that brought zir closer to the warrior just standing there in front of zir.

The warrior facing zir looked so confused Noalanon nearly laughed.

Obviously, that net was supposed to stop zir. Possibly drag zir to the ground.

The net started melting away, huge holes appearing in it as Noalanon walked on.

At first, the warrior took one step back, then a second, staring in horror. Then a determined look came over their face and they pulled a knife out.

The blade was steel, not black obsidian. Would it be able to cut zir skin?

The Bone Person swiped at Noalanon. Did they deliberately miss?

Ze slid to the side and kept walking away. Ze couldn't run, not and keep zir skin hardened. Ze walked past the Bone Person who took another swipe at zir and missed.

The remains of the net suddenly pulled tighter across zir chest, where it hadn't completely dissolved. Looking over zir shoulder, ze saw that the Bone Person had picked up the edges of the net and was trying to tug zir back.

Noalanon raised zir internal temperature higher and *pushed*. Ze took one deliberate step forward. Then another. And another.

The net tore with a satisfying *rip*.

The Bone Warrior slammed into zir back, trying to topple zir to the ground. Noalanon stumbled slightly and turned around so ze could watch the Bone Person, but ze kept walking anyway.

Ze wished yet again that ze could take another form, any form, that moved faster.

Determination filled the Bone Warrior's face. A quick glance told Noalanon that none of the Bone People had had any success; zir companions were still walking with zir.

Shouting, the Bone Warrior raised their blade and came at zir again. This time, Noalanon raised zir arm, deflecting the blow.

The steel bounced harmlessly off zir forearm.

The Bone Warrior struck at zir again and again, but they couldn't cut zir, or even bruise zir skin.

"What are you?" the Bone Warrior yelled in frustration. They couldn't knock Noalanon over. They couldn't cut zir. Their magical nets had failed.

Noalanon didn't bother replying, just kept walking backwards toward the gray wall. The coldness of the mist already tickled zir back.

The warrior stopped their attack when Noalanon stepped into the mist. Noalanon quickly turned around and started walking forward again.

However, now the wall fought zir.

The walk through the wall stretched forever. Noalanon knew that ze wasn't walking in a straight line. The first time through the wall ze had only gotten to the other side because of the presence of the Wind People behind zir, pushing zir forward.

If this wall was in the Stone People's territory, ze would have no problem walking through it. As it was, the winds confused zir, blew zir sense of direction around.

It was midday before Noalanon finally crossed out of the wall. Ze estimated that it had taken zir hours to make zir way through the wall.

Noalanon didn't see any of the other Stone People nearby, nor the cart that had brought them here. How far had ze wandered? Which direction should ze go? North? South? Ze didn't know. Ze cursed zir stone-sodden feet. It was so unlike a Stone Person to get lost! They almost always knew exactly where they were.

At least, in their own lands.

Taking a gamble, Noalanon turned north and started walking, determined not to stop until ze made it all the way back to Shan Yu, if necessary.

NOALANON DRAGGED ZIR FEET ALONG. They weren't sore. Not exactly. But ze had no strength left. It was as if the land itself now fought zir every step.

The sun had passed overhead and evening was coming. The cold didn't concern zir. However, zir energy was running low. Ze needed minerals to replenish what ze'd burned up earlier. There were stories of Stone People turning into solid rocks if they starved. While ze had always considered that a myth, at least in zir homelands, ze did wonder if there was an element of truth to them in foreign lands.

Ze needed to find the carts and zir people. Soon.

The smoke didn't bother the Stone People as much as it

appeared to bother the Wind People. It still irritated zir throat. Ze coughed now and again, trying to clear it.

Noalanon heard someone else coughing in the distance as twilight stole the color from the dried grass.

Ze walked toward the sound. Stone People could see better in the dark than any of the other People. However, the smoke still confused zir senses, making the tree trunks surrounding zir appear to loom as dark shadows, the roots sticking out just to trip zir.

Was that a fire up ahead? Ze walked slowly toward the light, cautious, fearful that it could be another trap.

Noalanon cried out with delight when ze saw Gan Ou sitting beside the fire, along with three other Wind People, as well as Daleki.

"Come, come," the Wind People said, bringing zir forward. Daleki took one look at zir and said, "Sit. I'll bring you minerals."

Noalanon gratefully collapsed. Finally! Ze could rest.

Daleki pushed a bowl under zir nose. Without bothering to use a spoon, Noalanon shoveled the minerals into zir mouth.

They crunched weirdly in zir mouth, but ze felt the strength and warmth of them flowing through zir quickly.

"Where are we?" Noalanon asked. "What happened to each of you?"

Gan Ou grimaced. "Old person here," she said. "More wily than those young folk, who got themselves captured in the Bone People's nets. Those nets are magic," she added with a shudder. "Made the others fall to the ground and pass out."

Noalanon nodded. That net *had* been meant to stop zir.

The other Wind People had similar stories of racing away before they'd gotten caught in the nets.

Daleki had a story that was close to Noalanon's, how ze had just walked away, the warriors being unable to stop zir.

"However, not all of the Stone People got away," Daleki warned. "When the warriors finally realized that they were no match for us one-on-one, they piled up on poor Hirshamin, forcing zir to the ground. I didn't…I couldn't stay. I couldn't help. I had to get away."

"You did the right thing," Noalanon said, reaching out and patting zir hand.

"But now what?" one of the Wind People, Yan Ji, asked. He sounded as young as he looked.

Gan Ou grimaced. "You three need to get back to the capital, or at least to the first messengers. Tell them what happened. That there's an army there on the other side of that wall, and they don't want to negotiate."

Noalanon shivered at the bleak tone in the old person's voice.

"And the rest of us?" Daleki asked.

"I'm going back in," Gan Ou said. "We don't leave people behind."

Noalanon blinked, surprised. Ze hadn't been expecting that response at all.

"Will you join me?" Gan Ou asked, giving first Noalanon, then Daleki, a hard stare.

"I will," Noalanon said.

Ze had come here to right a wrong. Yes, it was going to be a much larger task than ze had first anticipated.

Ze was not about to turn away now.

Chapter Twenty-One

SEA

"ISHKRA, we beg you, welcome our brother into your loving waters. Find Kaleenish worthy of your care. Wash away his pain, but let him keep the wisdom borne of such hurts. Let him be reborn soon so that he might share his knowledge with us yet again."

Ajooless took a deep breath and let it out with a sigh. Though she'd been to many funerals, this was the first one she'd ever conducted. However, as the representative of the main temple and an acolyte of Ishkra, the duty fell to her.

The remaining Sea People who traveled with her along the southern route through the mountains gathered around the large rock cairn that covered the body. They were only seventeen remaining, though they'd started with twenty. Two had turned back the first week, unable to endure the hardships of traveling.

Kaleenish had gone to sleep the night before and not woken up that morning. He'd been a gentle soul, a former teacher who had been to the foreign lands before, one of the few in their group. Ajooless would miss his wisdom, even though he'd been a male.

Ajooless placed a large white rock on the pile before stepping back and gesturing for the others to continue. Each person said something about Kaleenish's kindness or generosity, as was customary. When they were finished, they each placed one last rock on the cairn.

Usually a dead body was towed far out to sea and placed in a strong current that would carry the body away, the remains left in the ocean to feed the fish and plants there. If a person died of plague, they were burned.

The travelers had no stream to put the body in, and not enough wood this high up in the foothills on the eastern side of the mountains to build a pyre.

Ajooless tried to contain her impatience as the funeral went on. They needed to keep walking. They wouldn't cover many miles today. The day had dawned clear and bright, the blueness of the sky giving lie to how cold the air actually felt. It made all the Sea People sluggish until they started moving.

They were finally almost out of the foothills, however. Ajooless thought they were making good time. It was only a few days past midwinter. The people traveling along the northern route would only be reaching the capital of the Stone People by now, while her group would possibly reach the forests of the Wind People that afternoon, despite their late start that day.

Ajooless would be happy to get out of the mountains. They were pretty enough, she supposed, if you liked that kind of stark beauty. The dark green of the pines reminded her of the kelp beds of home. Wet grasses collected on the banks of the tiny creeks and streams they found smelled like the marshes, bitter, yet comforting. The rocks glared white in the bright sunlight, making her blink often. She hadn't known that the Sea People had an additional eyelid to protect their eyes from so much light. One of the older travelers had shown her the trick.

Finally, the last Sea Person said their goodbye and placed their rock on the cairn. Ajooless stepped forward, "Thank you for your kind words. I'm sure that Kaleenish's family will be happy with how he was honored and remembered, and that Ishkra won't turn Her face away from him as he swims through Her waters. Blessed be."

The others repeated the familiar phrase, "Blessed be."

Silence filled the area for a few awkward moments. Then Ajooless stepped away from the cairn, leading the group down the hill and back toward where they'd camped the night before.

When Ajooless realized that the rest of the group was still looking at her, she started issuing orders about breaking down the camp, getting moving. The others quickly followed her instructions, and they were on their way in less than an hour.

For the rest of the morning, Ajooless led the way along the path. It was well marked and well maintained, as the Stone People frequently traveled between the villages up higher in the foothills behind them and the next village below. In addition, once the trail had been created, mountain goats and sheep also used it, as it was easier than making their own path.

She generally led in the morning, switching off with older travelers in the afternoon.

Despite how the heavy backpack dug into her shoulders, and how tired her legs always felt, Ajooless didn't call a break until she could see the dark forests of the Wind People spreading out just below the foothills. As winter still reigned, they had to search for water every time they stopped.

Fortunately, that was something else that the travelers had learned about themselves—all of them were extremely good at locating water. Even just a trickle of melting snow could draw them. It had been one of Liseth's main worries, that the group wouldn't have enough water.

Despite Kaleenish's unexpected death, Ajooless suspected that the Sea People could survive on land much better than they realized, even land far from the rivers and streams of their home.

As Ajooless was finishing her portion of the midday meal—dried venison provided by the last village that they'd stopped at, as well as the flatbread the group had baked the night before—Hycineth came up. She stopped a few feet away and bowed low.

Ajooless contained her sigh. Despite how young she was, the other travelers treated her with great respect, leaving her alone for the most part. She did represent the high priestess and the temple. Sometimes she wished she could join in with them, but the group appeared to work better if she acted as the leader and remained aloof.

"What is it?" Ajooless asked Hycineth, who worked as a scout sometimes, traveling ahead of the group when the trail was uncertain.

"You need to come see," she said. She nodded, waited until Ajooless stood up, then hurried back the way she'd come.

Instead of going down along the trail, Hycineth led the way back up, to an outcrop of rock just above the traveler's heads. "That way," Hycineth said, pointing.

Ajooless shaded her eyes and blinked away the protective eyelid so she could see further.

Was that smoke in the distance? Rising above the dark trees?

"Fires?" Ajooless asked.

Hycineth shook her head. "It's too wet."

"Bone People," Ajooless said firmly.

The scout sat very still for a long moment before she nodded. "Aye. Probably. Bone People."

"Are there any waters nearby?" Ajooless said. "Where that smoke is rising?"

Hycineth opened her mouth then closed it again. "I don't know."

"Let's find out," Ajooless said, walking back to the rest of the group.

She might not be able to share where the headwaters of the Bone People lay. But she could certainly discover the origins of that smoke up ahead.

AJOOLESS WATCHED Mayleth touch the trickle of water flowing down the face of the nearby boulder, then marveled at how the older person's eyes turned all white as she looked within. Mayleth was one of the older Sea People on the journey, her skin starting graying and wrinkles forming around her eyes and the corners of her mouth. While many of the Sea People had begun wearing clothing that more resembled what the Wind and Stone People wore—shirts and pants—Mayleth still wore the long sleeveless dresses that worked as well in the waters as on land. Despite the heavy travel, this dress had remained pure white, shimmering in the sunlight against her gray-blue skin.

"There is a lake just behind the smoke, fed by underwater mountain streams," Mayleth announced, her voice sounding as if it were full of gravel.

All the travelers sat in a semi-circle in front of the fish traveler, as if she were a great teacher bringing them wisdom. Only Ajooless sat beside her, ready to help if necessary. The day had remained clear, the sunlight baking them despite the still cool air. None of them could detect the smell of smoke

—maybe it hadn't risen high enough for them to be able to smell it, or maybe they were still upwind of it.

Mayleth's eyes started to glow with a bluish light. "The fish are still in their winter stupor," she announced after a few moments. "I'm trying to wake one."

She blindly reached out with a hand, as if trying to grasp something she couldn't see.

Ajooless caught the seeking hand in her own. The older person immediately started squeezing Ajooless's hand tightly, as if trying to wring out any knowledge it might have.

Or maybe she was just seeking additional strength. Ajooless had to stop herself from fighting to free her hand as she felt her energy start to drain from her, tiredness washing over her like a gentle wave.

How was the older person doing that? Ajooless had never heard of someone with that sort of ability.

Except…there was the myth of Jukaless, who'd pursued the great sea monster across the ocean and back only because of the strength of her followers, who fell one by one as Jukaless took their strength.

"There," Mayleth said after a timeless while. Ajooless felt herself swaying, as if the core of her had been sucked out and just a translucent shell remained.

Suddenly, Ajooless *saw* what Mayleth did. The tiny silver minnow moved sluggishly, not wanting to leave the debris-filled shallow bottom of the lake. It swam slowly through the murky waters, its thin body giving the equivalent of a person's shivers as it passed through the colder layers.

Finally, the minnow made its way to the top of the lake. It took quite a push from Mayleth to force the fish up above the water. It lasted only a few moments in the clear air before it dove back down into the depths.

It was all that Ajooless needed.

Strange white people had stopped at the shoreline. It

appeared they were camped there. Their skin was as white as a bleached clam shell. They had strange blond hair.

Traveling with them was a skeleton—one of the elk, with its antlers protruding strangely in front of its face. It had burning red eyes and smoke rose up from its hooves. It stared out at the lake, as if it had seen the minnow raise its head.

It wasn't harnessed to a cart, so she wasn't sure of its purpose.

Except to strike dread into those who saw it.

But this wasn't a well-equipped war party, at least not as she understood it. This was a scouting mission. Maybe half a dozen people in all.

Mayleth pushed the minnow up above the water a second time. Ajooless reconfirmed her initial impressions, recounting heads and getting a better look at the camp before the fish dove back below the waters.

Surprisingly, Ajooless found that she could finally free her hand from the older person's grasp.

Ajooless gasped, as if she hadn't been breathing air for quite some time. She opened her eyes to face the group.

"I saw them," she announced, her voice sounding eerily like Mayleth's, almost feeling the gravel tickling her throat. "Half a dozen. Travelers. Scouts. With them…" Ajooless had to swallow down the bile that had risen. "With them was one of the elk. One of the dead elk. It traveled as a skeleton."

The rest of the group gasped. Mayleth nodded. "Aye. They're scouts. On their way across the mountains to the land of the Sea People."

"We have to tell the capital that they're coming," Ajooless said. They needed to send ambassadors out to greet these Bone People, to negotiate with them.

If it was possible to negotiate with a people who created skeletons as companions.

Ajooless pressed her lips together when she realized that

everyone was looking expectantly at her. They all expected *her* to come up with a plan.

She looked at the group. Should she split them up? Send some of them running back to the coast? Once they reached the streams and rivers of the Sea People's territory, they'd be able to travel much faster.

However, would it be fast enough? She had no idea how quickly the Bone People moved.

She glanced at Mayleth, who looked far grayer than usual. The older person appeared to be as exhausted as Ajooless felt. Neither of them was in any shape to travel more that day.

Hopefully, Mayleth would recover after a good night's sleep. Ajooless didn't want to have to conduct another funeral so quickly.

But what could they do? How to warn those back in the Sea People's territory? How to let them know that the Bone People were coming?

Ajooless tried not to label them as the enemy even in her own thoughts. However, there was a quality to them that set her teeth on edge, made her want to attack, like a shark smelling fresh blood.

So what was the plan?

Ajooless remembered how Mayleth had pulled Ajooless's strength to her, like Jukaless, the heroine of old.

If those stories were true, maybe the others were as well.

"Do you remember the stories of Gaynelus? The heroine of old?" Ajooless asked.

The travelers looked at each other, surprised, before finally Delayness replied. "Aye. She didn't just look out of the eyes of a fish, but could converse with those on shore using the creature."

Ajooless nodded. "Three of you need to race back over the mountains and to the territory of the Sea People. Use the waters when you can. Get news back to the capital that the Bone People are coming."

She saw confusion wash over them, as they'd obviously expected her to choose which ones would be in that group.

They needed to decide that among themselves, damn it! She didn't know who had the most strength or skill to make it back quickly.

"Two others of you need to go with Hycineth, the scout," Ajooless continued. "Your mission is to continue down the trail as fast as you can, then follow the camp of the Bone People. Learn everything about them. Never let yourselves be seen," Ajooless instructed.

She reminded herself yet again they weren't the enemy. And yet…

"And the rest of us, who remain here with you?" Delayness asked, obviously already having made her own decision.

"We're going to spend the next three days seeing if we can relearn the old lore and get a fish to talk. First one of the local ones, then find another, back in Shiboleth," Ajooless said. She looked out over the group. "I need the strongest with me, not the fastest. We will use your strength to power our magic."

Again, the group looked around at each other, uncertain what to do in the face of such absurdity. However, many of them appeared to catch a clue and nodded.

It took less time than Ajooless had expected for the groups to sort themselves out. The goodbyes were curt and abrupt, despite how close everyone had grown over the weeks of travel.

Ajooless had never seen such determination in the faces of her fellow travelers. Mostly, they'd glided along, content to be told what to do.

It filled her heart with a fierce joy, that when push came

to shove, her people could rise to the occasion. Even the most timid of them.

Ajooless and Mayleth spent the rest of the afternoon sleeping while the others set up camp, pitching their tents and cooking a large meal. In the morning, they'd start their quest, to find the magic of old and send a message back to the capital.

Before the scouts reached their location, and the conflict between their two People began.

MYTHS OF THE THIRD AGE

The Wind People's Creation Myth

IN THE BEGINNING, Sune Li danced alone in the dark. He/She decided to create companions and gave birth to Gan Zhur and Ban Zhur, the first two people. They asked for solid earth beneath their feet so that they could better dance for the God/Goddess. Sune Li called Kiproary out of the darkness, so that he/she could form the world. Kiproary called Ishkra out of the firmament, so that she could bring the forgetting rains and the waters of rebirth.

Sune Li set his/her lively spark deep in the heart of all living things, so that they might learn their true self and dance always in his/her light.

THE GOD/GODDESS of the Wind People goes by many names. Sune Li, God/Goddess of the flame/light is most common. But frequently the God/Goddess is called

Nameless One, the One God, the Lively One, Bringer of Light and Life.

Sune Li is not represented by any particular form, not embodied in any one creature. The God/Goddess may be represented by a carving of a flame, or a single candle, though in older times, was represented by a circle with radiating lines, representing the sun. But Sune Li is found in all light, not just sunlight.

As a soul ages, one of the goals for a Wind Person is to take every animal shape known, so as to be closer to Sune Li and achieve their own enlightenment, to move beyond physical form so they can just be a spirit, endless as a wind.

The Stone People's Creation Myth

Kiproary drifted in the darkness, a towering mountain in the blackness that existed before the stars. Ze awoke slowly, peering through the abyss and finding none to stare back. Kiproary looked behind Zir and started leaving a trail of bright lights for other to follow, once they took shape themselves. After many adventures, Kiproary decided to settle down. Ze formed the earth around Zir, setting Zir strength down into the core of the world, declaring this place and all the lands as sacred to Zir.

Kiproary created others like Zirself, tall and proud people who took to the firmament to grow. However, they were too static. They didn't move like the animals, but were more like the mountains. Kiproary found that while Ze could move around the stars, Zir people needed help to move on the earth.

So Kiproary invited Sune Li to follow Zir to the earth, to give all creatures movement. The people grew proud. To keep them humble, Kiproary also invited Ishkra and the waters of death and rebirth, as a reminder that the smallest trickle could cut a channel into stone over time, that even the tallest mountain could be reduced into pebbles eventually.

***

KIPROARY IS MOST OFTEN REPRESENTED by a drawing of a rounded hill. A sharp peak is considered ignorant, or arrogant, or both. Just a pebble placed on a table can sanctify a location. As well as sprinkling dirt finely ground from the holy mountain, where Kiproary first stepped down and walked the firmament.

The Sea People's Creation Myth

Ishkra floated with her siblings through the darkness until they formed the world, each placing their essence into the firmament so that life could begin.

The first people Ishkra birthed had no magic. They were solid as the mountains and as lively as the winds. But they were arrogant. They considered themselves the masters of all, and didn't respect the lives or light of others. They burned the forests, polluted the waters, carved the mountains into little pieces. And they warred with one another constantly, until finally, with the help of the gods, they destroyed themselves utterly. Thus ended the Age of Greed.

The second people Ishkra birthed were strictly a sea people. The waters were wide and plentiful, and the sea people had to live in harmony with their environment, learning quickly that they were dependent on the world and the waters.

But there were too many of them. Ishkra had favored them with multiple births, and they quickly ran out of space. They couldn't survive out of the water, and the gods turned their faces away from those who tried.

Diseases began to run rampant. Even their magic couldn't save them. Eventually, with the help of the gods, the people all died out. Thus ended the Age of the Sea.

The third people Ishkra birthed knew both land and sea. She let first Kiproary, then Sune Li, touch her pregnant belly, so that the Stone and Wind Peoples would be born as well. The Peoples were different, so they would live different lives in separate places. They all had magic, so they would see each other as equals. And they were all lively, so that they could dance and worship the gods.

Ishkra takes all souls and washes them clean at death, giving them another chance to live a pious life. The gods watch and wait, lest the people forget themselves, and decide to challenge the gods. If they do, the world will end in fire and all the Peoples, with the help of the gods, will die. Then the current age, the Third Age, will end.

ISHKRA IS REPRESENTED by a wavy line. Pure water will sanctify a space. Myths revolve around sincerely holy women who can do it through merely spitting. Knowledge and learning are valued above all. The Sea People have many more regular prayers during the day. Leading a pious life is more important to them than any of the other Peoples.

The Bone People's Creation Myth

Valtyr swam through his home, reveling in the absolute darkness. He needed no light, no firm ground, no water to bring him life. The abyss was everything. He needed nothing more.

Still, sometimes Valtyr was lonely. So He allowed others to form in the darkness: Sune Li, Kiproary, and Ishkra. But they didn't celebrate the darkness as He did. They disrespected their home, as well as the being who had allowed them to be born. They celebrated their own individual natures first and foremost, instead of relishing the dark like Valtyr did, or muchless respecting it and giving the abyss its well-deserved prayers.

So Valtyr banished them, sending them out of the darkness and onto the other side, away from the firmament and into the ether.

Occasionally, word of the others traveled across the abyss to Valtyr. It made Him happy to see His children thrive, though none of them acknowledged Him or His place as the greatest of all the gods.

But the Bone People, those who initially stayed behind with Valtyr in the darkness, learned the truth. They knew of the power of the abyss, the true power of death.

Eventually, after many adventures, the Bone People traveled from the abyss into the light, learned to live on the ground instead of swimming between the stars. Valtyr allowed them to be bathed in the waters of forgetfulness between births, though He forbade them to dance as the other Peoples.

The Bone People worshipped Valtyr every waking hour, knowing the absolute power of death over life, relishing the abyss and the dark places.

Valtyr heard the prayers of the other People, of the Wind and Stone and Sea People. Heard their boastfulness, heard their celebrations of light. Finally, He had had enough.

He sent great leaders to the Bone People, powerful leaders who could show them the way, to teach them to use the deaths of others to strengthen themselves.

Now, the Bone People have been called to right the wrongs paid to Valtyr, to show the other Peoples the error of their ways, to bring them all home to the darkness, to swim once again in the waters of the abyss.

Or to bring them death if they refuse.

VALTYR IS REPRESENTED by any sort of bone, though just a line across the dirt will do. All important prayers are done inside, in the dark. Dancing can be punished by death.

About the Author

Leah Cutter writes page-turning fiction in exotic locations, such as a magical New Orleans, the ancient Orient, Hungary, the Oregon coast, rural Kentucky, Seattle, Minneapolis, and many others.

She writes literary, fantasy, mystery, science fiction, and horror fiction. Her short fiction has been published in magazines like *Alfred Hitchcock's Mystery Magazine* and *Talebones*, anthologies like Fiction River, and on the web. Her long fiction has been published both by New York publishers as well as small presses.

Find Leah's books on Knotted Road Press at (www.KnottedRoadPress.com)

Follow her blog at www.LeahCutter.com.

Reviews

It's true. Reviews help me sell more books. If you've enjoyed this story, please consider leaving a review of it on your favorite site.

Come someplace new...

Are you a traveler? Do you enjoy exploring strange new worlds, new cultures, new people?

Journey into the various lands envisioned by Leah Cutter.

Sign up for my newsletter and I'll start you on your travels with a free copy of my book, *The Island Sampler*.

I will never spam you or use your email for nefarious purposes. You can also unsubscribe at any time.

http://www.LeahCutter.com/newsletter/

About Knotted Road Press

Knotted Road Press fiction specializes in dynamic writing set in mysterious, exotic locations.

Knotted Road Press non-fiction publishes autobiographies, business books, cookbooks, and how-to books with unique voices.

Knotted Road Press creates DRM-free ebooks as well as high-quality print books for readers around the world.

With authors in a variety of genres including literary, poetry, mystery, fantasy, and science fiction, Knotted Road Press has something for everyone.

Knotted Road Press
www.KnottedRoadPress.com